Harlequin Presents...

Other titles by

# ANNE HAMPSON

## IN HARLEQUIN PRESENTS



Other titles by

# ANNE HAMPSON

## IN HARLEQUIN ROMANCES

# ANNE HAMPSON

# the way of a tyrant

Harlequin Books

TORONTO • LONDON • NEW YORK • AMSTERDAM • SYDNEY

Harlequin Presents edition published December 1974
ISBN 0-373-70572-7

Second printing September 1977

Original hardcover edition published in 1974
by Mills & Boon Limited



Printed in Canada

# CHAPTER ONE

JANE COATES frowned in thought and remained silent for a long time before answering her brother's question.

'I can't, Les; I've told you this before, I'd like to help you, but the whole situation's far too involved.' She was sitting opposite to him at the breakfast table and her eyes were on the letter he had just a few moments ago picked up from the floor in the hall.

'It's not involved at all. In fact, to my way of thinking it couldn't be more simple. We've no parents to consider. We can just give the house into an agent's hands to rent for us – we don't want to sell it at this stage – not until we've decided if we can settle there.'

'I'm not thinking of that part of it. It's the deceit, Les I'm not much good at it, as you know.'

Encouraged by the unmistakable lack of emphasis in his sister's tones, Les continued to press his point.

'Who is there to know we're not husband and wife? This hotel of which I'm offered the management is only one of a whole chain of luxury hotels in the West Indies, so I'm sure no one is going to come along and delve into my private life – not once this initial business is transacted.'

Jane secretly agreed about this but, speaking her thoughts aloud, she said,

'Are you quite sure it's all off with Carolyn? I mean, isn't she tempted by the prospect of living in Barbados?'

Impatiently Les shook his head.

'Apparently she never really was serious; I took too much for granted. When I applied for the post I was confident that I could comply with the condition that I must be married. I was staggered when Carolyn refused me.'

Memory flooded in at this point and Jane smiled faintly to herself. Scott Kingsley had also received a shock, four years ago, when she herself had refused his proposal of marriage. The trouble with men, she decided, was that they always did take too much for granted, assuming that girls were falling over themselves to enter the state of wedded bliss. That might have been the case at one time, but not now, not since the advent of female independence. Of course, with Scott there had been a very good reason for her refusal of his offer, and again Jane smiled on recalling her outright declaration that he was not her type; that he possessed too little strength of character, was altogether too gentle and pliable, and she had no use for a man whom she could twist around her little finger.

Jane's musings were halted as her brother began speaking again, persuasively. He could not give up the post, he said. It was the chance of a lifetime, and as for Jane herself, she would have a marvellous time, for she loved the sun and the sea, and there would be ample opportunity for her to enjoy these on the lovely coral island of Barbados.

'My job,' she murmured rather absently. She was picturing the life she would have and admitting that it was more than a little enticing.

'You've been complaining for months that it's not the same since the coming of this new boss of yours.

Only last week you were saying you'd look for another post.'

This was true. Mr. Horsefield was so very different from Mr. Grant, whose retirement had resulted in the coming of the new office manager. Mr. Horsefield spent most of his time finding fault with the methods of his predecessor, and with those who had worked under him.

'I'll think about it,' Jane agreed at last. 'But don't be too optimistic. I like the idea of living on the island, but I do not like the idea of the deception.'

Les shrugged and repeated that no one was going to come along and delve into his private life.

'The climate's perfect,' he added, still pressing her. 'As much sun as you'll ever want, but rain too, just to keep the vegetation lush and green. And there are the trade winds to keep you cool. They blow all the time.'

Jane's full, pretty lips curved in a smile.

'You've been busy,' she observed in some amusement.

'Naturally. Right from the moment I applied for the post.'

'What exactly would I have to do?' she wanted to know, reaching for the toast. 'Surely I must do more than talk nicely to the guests, as you at first told me?'

Les shook his head.

'No, that's all you have to do. Just stroll around and look beautiful – that shouldn't be much trouble,' he added, and received a darkling frown for his flattery.

'It's a wonder the people who interviewed you didn't want to see your wife.'

'I told them I wasn't yet married.' He paused a

moment before venturing to inform her that she would be required to accompany him to Mr. Spender's house that evening. 'Mr. Spender is the man who interviewed me in London, as you know,' he added, watching her face intently for any signs of a swift refusal. 'He's written to say he wants to see my wife.'

'This evening?' Automatically she shook her head. 'I can't, Les . . . I'm sorry.'

'Scared – you?' he exclaimed. 'I don't believe it! You've never been scared in your life.'

Jane received that unsmilingly. It was the truth. In fact, it was owing to her own strength of character that she had turned Scott down. Fearless herself, she had no time for a man who was forever giving in to her every whim simply because he was afraid of incurring her displeasure. Had he asserted himself, displayed a little mastery, letting her know that she was not always to have her own way, then the affair might have ended differently.

'It's the deceit,' she repeated on realizing that Les was awaiting her reply. 'I don't like it at all.' He said nothing and she went on, 'This evening . . . am I to pose as your wife or your fiancée?' She saw his face clear and once again warned him not to be too optimistic. She would consider the matter during the day and ring him at his work later in the afternoon.

'You're to pose as my wife.'

A heavy frown crossed the high unlined brow, and her large hazel eyes took on an accusing light.

'You've lied – said you're married already?'

Reluctantly he nodded.

'Mr. Spender rang me soon after the interview asking the date of my forthcoming marriage. It was clear that I was well in the running for the post, so I gave him a date – which was a week last Saturday.'

Jane's frown deepened, but she refrained from speaking any word of censure to her brother. He had set his heart on working abroad ever since deciding on hotel management as a career, and this post was the fifth for which he had applied, the other four having been given to older men. This particular post had come his way owing to the recommendation of David Shore who, with his wife Susan, managed the Carib Palm Hotel at Bathsheba, on the east coast of the island. So well had they improved the hotel that they were held in high esteem by the West Indies hotel company and in consequence David's recommendation had been been taken seriously by Mr. Spender, the man responsible for interviewing the applicants in London. Les's failure to obtain the post would be a bitter disappointment to the Shores as well, thought Jane, who, with her brother, had been very friendly with David and Susan before they went off to live in Barbados three years previously.

'I'll have to go.' Glancing at the clock, Les rose from the table. 'Don't let me down, Jane,' he begged before leaving the house five minutes later.

She said nothing; her eyes brooded as she watched him back the car along the drive. Normally he lived at the hotel at which he worked, but he had had a week's holiday which he naturally spent with Jane, the house being owned by them jointly. She herself had had a week off work, but was due back now, and as the car turned at the end of the drive she followed her routine and went into the kitchen to wash the dishes. Leaving them to drain, she ran upstairs to make her bed before putting on her coat, grabbing her handbag and dashing off to catch her bus.

'Jane – hi there!'

'Hello, Doris.' Jane sat down beside the acquaintance who had hailed her. 'Are you working? I thought you'd left when you got married?'

'I did leave, but we couldn't manage on Keith's money, so here I am, a working girl again.'

'It's difficult on one salary,' agreed Jane, settling back against the upholstery. 'How is Keith these days? I heard he'd been promoted.'

'That's right, but we still can't manage. By the way, is Les going to work in Barbados, or somewhere in that direction?'

'He's got a post there, yes.'

'When's he going?'

'It isn't settled yet, Doris, so I can't say anything about it.'

'You mean he might not accept the post?'

'We're not sure.' Jane spoke rather abruptly, wondering that news could travel so swiftly, and so far.

'If he does go you'll miss him. You should have got married when you had the chance.'

Jane turned her head, eyes glinting.

'How do you know I had the chance to get married?'

'Well, to be honest I didn't know for sure. But that fab man – Scott Kingsley – was so obviously in love with you that anyone could see he'd propose. He did, didn't he?'

Jane pursed her lips. Nothing vexed her more than for her private affairs to become public. But Doris and Keith had been at two staff dinner dances when Jane had had the honour of the unceasing attention of the nephew of one of the directors of another firm, and as this man at twenty-six was by far the most distinguished person present it was only to be expected that tongues would wag.

'Scott and I had nothing in common,' said Jane abruptly in reply to her companion's question. 'He was not my type.'

A small silence followed. Doris seemed hesitant at first, but her curiosity got the better of her and she said,

'Rumour had it that he was a broken man when you refused him—'

'Broken man? Nonsense!' Lacking in strength he might be, but Scott Kingsley had never struck her as being *that* weak. 'I never heard anything so ridiculous!'

'He went off somewhere,' persisted Doris. 'No one has ever heard of him since you and he parted.'

'Parted isn't the apt word,' Jane almost snapped. 'Scott and I were never going steady.'

'You did go out with him, though, Jane. You were often seen in his car.'

'We dined a few times, and danced. But there was never any question of my being serious with him.'

'But Scott . . .? He was serious – at least, everyone got that impression.'

Impatiently Jane sighed. It was a strange thing, but she very much resented the rumour which put Scott in the position of rejected lover. True, he was not her type, but he was a charmer for all that, with his incredible height and broad shoulders and handsome features. His brown hair waved attractively, his smoky blue eyes were frank and deep-set and they could come alive with laughter if something struck their owner as being funny.

'This is my stop.' Thankfully Jane rose and, nodding faintly and managing a smile, she left her companion without having to continue a conversation which she found more than a little irritating.

However, the conversation remained with her and after frowningly going over it as she walked the quarter of a mile or so through the back streets towards the wide square in which her office was situated, she found herself thinking more about the man who had so wanted to marry her. He had in the first instance appeared from nowhere, being unconnected with the firm giving the staff dance. One or two people of Jane's acquaintance had heard of the father, who owned a chain of shoe shops throughout the country. It was rumoured that Scott and his father had disagreed owing to Scott's refusal to enter the business.

On first setting eyes on Jane he was quite plainly attracted to her and by the end of the first staff dance he had made a date with her. There followed a short period of friendship during which Jane became acutely aware that her every whim was being pandered to by the man whose physique and noble bearing should instantly have branded him the type with great strength. In fact, it had amazed Jane that she could get all her own way with him, and it had also disappointed her in some strange fashion, the reason for which completely eluded her. That she was proud to be seen with him there was no doubt at all. He attracted stares by his height and looks and air of distinction. He had poise and confidence and commanded respect wherever he went. All this was so contradictory to the fact of his being so soft and pliable with Jane. It was as if, where women were concerned, he did not dare assert any authority. He had been as wax in her hands and she knew for sure that, had she married him, his weakness would very soon have palled. Not that there had been any question of her accepting his offer, since Jane's innate caution had prevented her from falling in love with him – or even becoming attracted in a way that would result in hurt at the parting.

How well she recalled that day when, having driven her to the seaside in his car, he had taken her on to the beach and, after the quiet stroll and the equally quiet rest on a seat under the shade of a bright umbrella, had asked her to marry him.

His expression when she had refused! Jane would never forget his astonishment and disbelief.

'I love you, Jane, and I could have sworn you felt the same way about me.' That he had little or no experience of women was made patently clear; Jane had suspected this from the first – and not for her was the inexperienced male. There was so much to learn about women, and in her opinion a man should have done something about this before deciding to marry. 'Are you really refusing me?'

'I'm afraid so, Scott. I'm sorry—'

'Sorry!' For the first time she saw the fringe of his temper, but only the fringe. He hadn't even the ability to become angry at her decision. 'Why, Jane, are you refusing me? At least you can tell me that.'

What must she say to him? She told him the truth, that he was not her type, at which he had frowned in puzzlement and asked to know what her type of man happened to be.

She was in a quandary. How could she tell him he was too soft, too pliant by far? She had been able to order him about – or nearly so; deliberately she had experimented, refusing to dine where he suggested they dine.

'I prefer the Grand,' she said rather haughtily on one occasion, and the instant response had been,

'Then that's where you shall go, my dear.'

The swift capitulation had left her contemptuous ... but oddly disappointed as well. What kind of a man was he to allow himself to be overridden every time? How awful to find oneself married to a spineless jellyfish!

In the end Jane was driven, by Scott's persistence, to tell him openly that he lacked the strength of character which she would need for her own happiness. Amazed, he had said,

'I always believed a woman desired gentleness in her husband?'

She had been a little time finding a reply to this.

'Well, yes, she does, in a way. But she also wants to be forced to look up to him. He must have a certain – er – mastery about him—' Jane had stopped and shrugged her shoulders. 'This is painful for us both, Scott, and so let's drop the matter. It was nice knowing you, but this is the end.' Jane thought he flinched; she heard him repeat,

'It was nice knowing you,' bitterly and with the merest sign of a glint in those deep blue eyes. 'Thanks!' He paused a moment, frowning. She felt instinctively that he was asking himself how he had come to fail. 'You've said, in effect, that I'm a weakling. You've also hinted that I've no experience of women.'

Protestingly she shook her head, but was told not to bother about tact; it was a little late anyway, he added in the same bitter tones.

'Please, Scott, do as I ask and let the matter drop,' she begged, embarrassed and also filled with a sense of guilt. She had never liked hurting people, and she knew she had hurt Scott exceedingly.

'Very well.' He looked at her and she saw the brooding expression in his eyes, the sort of expression that tells plainly of an ache that touches the heart. He was young for his twenty-six years, she thought. Had she herself been seventeen it might have been all right, but she was twenty, and full of confidence and self-assurance and a knowledge of what she required in the man she would eventually marry.

Scott Kingsley left far too much to be desired.

On reaching her office Jane was caught up in other matters and Scott's image vanished from her mind. But it returned at lunch time, for no apparent reason, and she found herself wondering what had happened to him. His father having died soon after Jane had rejected him, Scott had sold out to a famous shoe company and it was rumoured that he had said he was going to find something more interesting than shoes in which to invest his money.

And then he had disappeared. Jane had heard nothing of him for four years, but, strangely, his face was still as clear as ever; she could see it plainly just whenever she decided to bring it to mind.

How little they had known of each other, really. Les had been working in Scotland, where he managed an hotel in Edinburgh, so although Scott had known of his existence he had never met the brother of the girl he wanted to marry. Jane had never met Scott's father or the sister he mentioned now and then, a woman ten years his senior who had married an American and lived in Detroit.

By now, Jane surmised, Scott would be married, since he was handsome enough to attract ninety-nine women out of a hundred, and since he himself obviously desired to be married, having known Jane a mere five weeks before proposing to her.

'Coming for a stroll, Jane?' Beryl, one of her colleagues, popped her head round the door and brought Jane's musings up with a jerk. 'It's a lovely day; let's have ten minutes or so in the sun.'

'All right.' Rising at once, Jane picked up her handbag and left the office with Beryl. They had covered a mere couple of hundred yards when Beryl's foot slipped off the pavement and she overbalanced, grabbing at Jane for support. A passing car glanced against Beryl, but although Jane also fell into the roadway she picked herself up immediately, unhurt. A crowd swiftly gathered and the driver, having helped Jane to get Beryl to her feet, told both girls to get into the car.

Ten minutes later they were at the hospital, where Beryl was detained.

'Can you take me back to my office?' Jane was asking the car driver as they left the hospital together. 'My boss will be fuming already.'

'I'm sorry, but I'm in a hurry. This business has wasted enough of my time,' and without waiting to hear what Jane might have to say to that he turned on his heel and strode over to where he had parked his car.

It was half past two when Jane entered the office; Mr. Horsefield had given instructions that she and Beryl present themselves to him immediately on their return. He was sitting like a judge behind his desk and Jane's heart sank when she noticed his expression. And as she suspected, he had no wish to listen to her explanation. He had no patience with lateness, he kept on interrupting to tell her. She should have started work at two o'clock.

'Yes, Mr. Horsefield, I know,' she said, trying to be patient. 'But as I've told you, Miss Ponting fell and was hit by a car—'

'You weren't hit, though. Why should you be late?'

'I had to go to the hospital with her. Mr. Horsefield.'

'Why?' Pale blue watery eyes peered at her from over the top of rimless spectacles. 'It was just an excuse, wasn't it – going off to the hospital when there was no need?'

'Miss Ponting couldn't go on her own. She was suffering from shock.'

'I thought you said the car driver took her to the hospital?'

'Yes, he did.'

'Then she wouldn't have been alone, would she? Miss Coates, I've let it be known, over and over again, that I'm not running this office as it has been run up till now. There was not an atom of efficiency in the whole place.' He leant back and tapped the blotter with a ruler. 'I'm making an example of you, Miss Coates. You'll take a week's notice as from Friday.'

Her eyes blazed, but she said nothing. That evening

she accompanied her brother to the home of Mr. Spender, where she was received graciously and told she would be a great asset to her husband in his new post as manager of the Coral Gables Hotel in Barbados.

Jane was on the beach, clad in a bikini. Already she had acquired a lovely golden tan and this contrasted with the lighter gold of her hair, hair that fell in a gleaming mass on to her shoulders, forming a glorious cloak. She looked the picture of health as she stood there, graceful as the tall coconut palm against which she leant, her hands at the back of her, pressed against the trunk. She had been in the water, then dried herself on the pale sands where others had also exposed their bodies to the sun. It was tea time now and the private beach of Coral Gables was almost deserted. A mere few people remained, under a clump of palms farther along the shore, but just where Jane was the sands were deserted completely. Her dreamy gaze rested on the fringe of blue water lapping the shore, with scarcely a murmur. What a tropical paradise the island had turned out to be! It was heavenly! Coral sands and palm trees; exotic sweetly-perfumed flowers; people who were noted for their friendliness and hospitality . . .

Her attention was suddenly arrested by the man coming towards her – what a tall man, she thought, and he was swinging along with such ease and grace that he might not have been touching the sands at all. He wore shorts and a short-sleeved shirt, with sandals on his feet. He had come from the hotel, obviously, for otherwise he would not be on the beach . . .

Her flesh tingled all at once and a gasp of disbelief escaped her.

'Scott!' she breathed long before he reached her. 'It can't be!'

He would have passed by, but on glancing her way as he came abreast of her he stopped, just as astonished as she by this unexpected meeting.

'Jane!' He could only stare for a long moment into her lovely face, a face of strength and great character, of finely-modelled features and exquisite contours. 'How did you get here?'

She was faintly embarrassed, but at the same time she was able to take in the remarkable changes that the four years had wrought in him. He had acquired lines she did not particularly care for; his mouth was not so full and generous, those blue eyes held a distinctly cynical light. The jawline spelled implacability and even his voice was firmer than she remembered it, and it contained an edge of austerity she would never for one moment have associated with the man who had always been so eager to please, to pander to her every whim.

'I'm at the hotel,' she managed at length, forcing a smile to her lips.

'So you're on holiday too. Well, well, what a coincidence!' He continued to stare down into her face. 'How long have you been here?'

She hesitated, aware of an uneasiness sweeping over her. She fidgeted and in so doing her wedding ring was revealed.

'I'm not on holiday—'

'You're married?' Scott's eyes were on the ring and as she watched a sneer curved the thin line of his lips. It caused her to start in surprise, so at variance was it with the man she had once known. 'And did you manage to find your ideal – the strong man with the dictatorial traits so essential for your happiness?'

Jane coloured.

'I'm sorry if I hurt you, Scott,' she began, but he immediately interrupted her.

'Hurt? I was merely amused, once I had thought about it. You haven't answered my question. Did you find this masterful tyrant under whose subjection you were to discover such ecstatic bliss?'

The colour in Jane's cheeks deepened with anger. Civility was too difficult to summon.

'You're insulting, Scott,' she flashed. 'Such sarcasm amounts to downright rudeness!'

The censure passed over him; he was immune to it and Jane was finding it hard to believe that this was the man who had been so gentle and kind, and so meek. Not by any stretch of imagination could she visualize his being meek now . . . quite the contrary, in fact.

'I take it your husband's with you?' The fine timbre of his voice was edged with curiosity.

'I – er – yes, he is.' This came out slowly, as she grappled uneasily for some way of voicing the deliberate lie which hung on her lips. How difficult it was to tell Scott an untruth. This first week at Coral Gables had run so smoothly that already she had reached a state of pleasant complacency over the matter of her false position as wife to the manager of the hotel. But now she was placed awkwardly, knowing full well that her 'husband' must come into the picture. 'He's – he's the manager of Coral Gables,' she informed him, rejecting the temptation to be perfectly frank and disclose the fact of the deception, explaining that the necessity for it arose by the refusal of Les's girl-friend to marry him.

'The—!' Scott broke off immediately and his eyes took on the most odd expression. He turned away, appearing to be interested in the group of people farther along the beach. The avoidance of her eyes was deliberate and for Jane it had some disquieting significance. 'You didn't change your name on your marriage.' Scott spoke thoughtfully, his abstracted gaze on her fingers, which were playing nervously on the trunk of the tree against which she was standing. She found this avoidance of her eyes most puzzling. It would almost seem that he wished to allay any fears she might have; although aware of the absurdity of this idea Jane could not rid herself of it. It suddenly filled her with trepidation which, on the surface, was totally unnecessary. But Jane was experiencing something beneath the surface – something vague yet troublesome. 'Coates is not a common name by any means.' Soft tones and edged with an indefinable quality that set Jane's nerves quivering. There was something actually chilling about Scott in this unfathomable mood.

'When did you arrive?' she asked, hoping to divert him.

'About an hour ago.'

'You didn't book in beforehand.' She wondered just how she would have felt had he done so and, on glancing through the book, she had noticed his name there, as one of the expected guests. This thought led naturally to another question, one that escaped involuntarily. 'You're alone?'

An almost imperceptible trace of a smile touched his mouth.

'I'm quite alone.' A small pause and then, 'Were you wanting to know if I'm married?'

Additional colour leapt to her cheeks.

'Of course not! Why should I be interested?'

Scott shrugged his shoulders.

'No particular reason,' he agreed carelessly. 'I just thought your question might have an underlying inquiry.' Another pause. His satirical smile was a prelude to words of amused contempt. 'I found after all that marriage wasn't necessary. Why should a man take on the responsibility when he can have all the perks without?' She made no answer, naturally, and he added, 'I have you to thank for turning me down, Jane. I shall be eternally grateful.' Still no comment from Jane. His satirical voice continued, 'Marriage is a much overrated institution – unnecessary except for the highly romantic.'

Jane said at last, shaking her head in disbelief,

'You've changed, you used to be so . . . so . . .' Her words trailed off, for she could never be so outspoken with this man as she was with the Scott Kingsley she had known four years ago.

'So weak and lacking in mastery,' he said, and now his voice was brusque and clipped. 'I trust the change is for the better?'

'You're cynical,' she said, and he immediately inclined his head in agreement.

'Cynicism is bred of experience.' A taunting smile appeared in those deep-set blue eyes. 'Your husband—' Abruptly he changed the subject, and his expression also underwent a change, becoming once again unfathomable. 'Your husband . . . he didn't strike me as the dominant driving type. I hope you haven't been disappointed?'

She swallowed hard, trying desperately to recall

whether or not she had ever mentioned her brother's Christian name to him. She supposed she must have done and could only hope he had forgotten it by now. It was boldly printed on the brochures and should he not have forgotten then surely he would begin to suspect something. Of course, she told herself, it did not really matter if he did. He was only a guest and would be gone soon anyway. She asked how long he was thinking of staying at the hotel and received the laconic reply,

'Until I'm ready to leave.'

Jane felt she had been snubbed and lowered her head in confusion. It seemed inconceivable that Scott could make her feel so uncomfortable, Scott whom she had secretly dubbed a spineless jellyfish!

'Where are you living now?' she asked as the long silence became unbearable. 'I heard you had left your father's house after he'd died.'

He made no immediate reply; his eyes swept the shore, but in a casual way, just as if he were used to exotic scenes such as this.

'I sold up the home in England,' was all he offered, and Jane moved uncomfortably, aware that once again she had been snubbed.

'I must go in now,' she murmured, stooping down for the wrap she had dropped on the sand at her feet.

He looked oddly at her.

'You help your husband, I presume?'

She nodded.

'Just a little. There isn't a great deal for me to do.'

'No? I should have thought the management of a place like Coral Gables was a joint effort?'

'I talk to the guests,' she said, drawing a circle in the sand with her foot. 'We both dine with them every evening.'

'It must be a pleasant post for you.'

She nodded, beginning to move away.

'It is. We were lucky to get it – at least my husband was. I really had nothing to do with it in the first place.'

A silence hung; she edged a little farther away and he followed.

'How long have you been married?'

'Not long.' She frowned to herself, wishing she had made her escape sooner. 'My husband had to be married in order to obtain the post.'

'Your husband ...' musingly. She caught her breath, fearing he had guessed why she had not referred to Les by his Christian name. 'You haven't told me how long you've been married?'

'Just a few weeks. We've been at Coral Gables for only a week.' Jane increased her pace. 'I'll leave you to your stroll,' she said pointedly, but Scott fell into step beside her.

'I'm returning to the hotel myself,' he said pleasantly, and she had no alternative than to allow him to walk along beside her.

# CHAPTER TWO

THE impact of the unexpected meeting with Scott was felt by Jane for a long while, and after bathing and dressing she went in search of her brother, who was in his office, as she expected. Looking up, he smiled, then frowned a little on noticing her expression.

'Is anything wrong?' he inquired before she could speak.

Closing the door behind her, she came towards his desk.

'How long is Mr. Kingsley staying with us?'

Her brother's frown deepened.

'I've no idea. Is it important?'

She hesitated.

'I used to know him, back in England. We went out together for a little while.' She paused a moment, reluctant to worry Les, and yet she had to speak about her fears. 'He asked me to marry him—'

'He did? You never mentioned anything about a proposal of marriage.'

'I refused him; we weren't suited. However, what's worrying me is that he might have guessed that you and I are not husband and wife.' She went on to explain fully, and even as she spoke her uneasiness grew. 'I know he can't do anything to harm you,' she ended, 'but I shall be glad when he's gone.'

'You mentioned me to him – four years ago?'

'Of course. And I expect I referred to you as Les, but he could possibly have forgotten your name after all this time.'

Les automatically fingered a hotel brochure lying on his desk. His name, as manager, was printed on it: 'Mr. Leslie Coates.' Les gave a small sigh.

'It's unfortunate that you and he know each other, but as you say, he can't do anything to harm me – and in any case, I can't see that he would want to.' He glanced at Jane inquiringly and she nodded.

'I'm worrying unnecessarily,' she admitted, but repeated that she would be glad when he had gone.

'I don't suppose he'll stay long, being on his own.'

'No, probably not.' She saw that her brother was already occupying himself with one of the papers before him, writing slowly and thoughtfully. 'I'll go,' she said, turning to the door. 'I'll see you at dinner time.'

The dining-room was thickly-carpeted with shaded lights and flowers everywhere. Some of the tables were set in arched alcoves while others were spaced along the two shorter walls. A space in the centre of the room was left for dancing, and on a raised dais at the far end of the room the steel band played soft West Indian music.

Jane and her brother sat with an American family, while across from them, at a table for one, sat Scott. He had sent Jane a faint smile on entering and then his attention appeared to be wholly on what was going on around him. In fact, thought Jane, he appeared more than ordinarily interested, and she wondered if he were feeling rather lost, sitting there, all on his own.

But after a while he rose and the next minute he was dancing with one of the two English girls who had come in only a few hours previously. The couple were soon in conversation, Jane noticed, unable to take her eyes off Scott, whose height dominated the small space on which several other couples were dancing. No diffidence such as Jane had known; no sign of any lack of confidence. Just the contrary; Scott Kingsley just oozed dignity and self-assurance. As she watched, with a strange feeling of fascination, Jane saw his mouth curve with a cynical smile; she saw his eyes look down at his partner's face and take on an expression of what could only be described as contempt. What had the girl said to cause this reaction? Jane wondered, suddenly flushing as Scott, becoming aware of her fixed regard as her eyes travelled with him round the dance space, gave her a wide stare and at the same time lifted one eyebrow, arrogantly.

Jane lowered her lashes and concentrated on the food on her plate. The conversation got under way and for the next hour she determinedly kept her eyes away from the man at the next table.

However, just as the meal was ending he came to her and she was forced to dance with him. Her brother caught her eyes as she rose, and as all he did was to grin faintly it was clear that he had no anxieties regarding the deceit he was practising.

The poised assurance that Scott had displayed when dancing with the other girl was very much in evidence when after a few moments had passed he casually remarked on her dancing.

'Still as light as ever, Jane.'

'Thank you.'

'I haven't noticed your husband dancing.'

'He doesn't dance.'

'No? But he should, as manager of the hotel. There'll be many women who come here alone, and it's part of his job to see that they're entertained.' There seemed to be an undertone of sharpness in his voice which startled Jane. She opened her mouth to ask what it had to do with him and then closed it again, remembering that he was a guest.

'My husband has never liked dancing,' was all she said, and changed the subject. 'Have you been to Barbados before?'

No answer for a space and then,

'Yes. I know the island well.'

'You do? Have you stayed here before – at this particular hotel?'

Scott nodded.

'I've stayed at several hotels on the island, including this one.'

'We have friends managing the Carib Palm Hotel at Bathsheba. Have you stayed there?'

'I have.'

Jane glanced up into his face. She caught a strange glance and was also in time to see his face break into a self-satisfied smile. It was quite absurd, she told herself, but she had the impression that Scott Kingsley was thoughtfully planning something . . . something which would react upon herself. Impatiently she shook off the feeling. The incredible change in the man was unnerving, she decided, and that was the reason for these odd sensations that kept troubling her. He was deeper, somehow, and unfathomable. There was an air of mystery about him, and she wondered what he did for a living.

'It was rumoured that you hadn't kept your father's

business on,' she ventured when at length her curiosity could no longer be held in check. 'Are you in some other kind of business?'

A glimmer of amusement entered his eyes.

'Yes,' he told her, 'I am in some other kind of business.'

A non-committal reply, and she was no more knowledgeable now than before putting her question. There had been a sort of dry mockery in his tones that quelled her and she remained silent until the music stopped and Scott accompanied her to her table.

'Thank you,' he said, 'I enjoyed our dance together.'

'So did I.' Her smile was a forced attempt which seemed to afford him amusement, for that glimmer appeared in his eyes again.

'We'll probably meet again later,' he said, and left her.

She became inexplicably tensed and it was a relief when she was able to leave the restaurant and go to her room, where she remained for a short while, trying to relax. Why should she be feeling like this – actually afraid of Scott and yet without any valid reason? He was only a guest, and would be gone shortly, and it was most unlikely she and he would ever meet again – unless he came to the hotel on a future occasion, which she sincerely hoped would not be the case.

At last she went down to the lounge and then out to the terrace where a steel band played beneath a brightly-coloured canopy. All around grew the luxurious tropical vegetation which formed part of the extensive gardens of the hotel. The guests, women in evening gowns and men in white jackets, sat at glass tables on which candles burned in coloured jars. Native waiters, white-coated and erect, moved silently between the tables, their teeth flashing in the dim light as they smilingly served the drinks. Below, the palm-fringed shore curved away towards a small rocky outcrop; the dark translucent waters were gently lapping the beach. From somewhere in the grounds of the hotel there drifted the heavy scent of the frangipani tree, blown by the cooling trade wind breeze coming in from the north-east.

As was her duty Jane moved around, sitting for a few minutes at one table or another, chatting and smiling and answering questions. She had automatically looked for Scott, but as he was nowhere to be seen she assumed he was either in one of the smaller lounges or in the bar. His room was directly above her as she strolled back through the grounds; she glanced up, but there was no light. She avoided the bar and the lounges and was just congratulating herself that she had managed to escape contact with Scott when, having gone outside again in order to enjoy a few quiet minutes before going to bed, she quite literally bumped into him on turning into one of the lonely tree-shaded paths that wound about in the grounds.

'Oh . . . I'm sorry . . .' Her words died unfinished as her arms were caught in his hands. The contact evoked memories as emotions sprang to the alert and she realized with a shock that it was not only his face that had remained clearly with her during those four years but the memory of his touch as well. The secret admission brought rosy tints to her cheeks, and a slow smile curved Scott's lips as he contemplated her for a long moment before saying,

'Where are you off to at this time of the night?'

'I was just taking a stroll.' Jane twisted away as his grip on her arms slackened. Confused by her feelings, she averted her head, but not before she had noticed the searching glance he directed at her.

'All alone? Why isn't your husband with you? After all, you're still on your honeymoon – or should be.' The softly-spoken words drifted out on a wave of satirical amusement and her colour deepened.

'He's busy with the guests,' she said shortly, and would have moved on, but Scott's body swerved, barring her way.

'A stickler for duty, eh?' An undertone of sarcasm now, and Jane's chin lifted.

'It's his job to look to the guests,' she snapped. 'My – husband's always put his job before anything else!' She had almost made a slip and said 'brother's', but on looking up into Scott's dark countenance she was relieved to note that the hesitation had escaped him ... or had it? Nerves tingled as she remembered his deliberate avoidance of her eyes on two previous occasions. She had gained the impression that he had wished to allay any fears she might have. Was it possible that he had guessed at the deception but was not intending to make his knowledge known to her? She shook her head in a gesture of bewilderment and dismissed the idea as being too absurd to be true.

Scott was saying in some amusement,

'So your husband puts duty before anything else? What an accommodating wife you turned out to be.'

Bright spots of colour portrayed her rising anger; it tinted her cheeks and even in the dim light it was discernible to Scott's contemplative eyes.

'I find your remarks insulting,' she flashed. 'My affairs are private, and therefore I'll request you not to comment on them!'

His eyes sharpened; the amusement faded as his manner changed.

'Is this the way you usually speak to the guests?' he inquired softly.

'The guests don't usually insult me!'

A long silence followed as Scott looked at her, his forehead creased as if he were in a state of indecision.

'Perhaps,' he said at last, 'I'd better tell you who I am. I meant to inform your husband at the first opportunity, but as he appeared to be very busy I decided that tomorrow would do.' Scott paused a moment and a faint smile touched his lips as he noted the sudden pallor that crept into her cheeks. 'It appears that you've already guessed who I am?' But Jane shook her head vigorously, as if she would repel the staggering revelation before it assumed any clear form. 'I'm your boss, Jane,' he then said quietly. 'I thought it best to tell you before you treated me with further disrespect.'

'My . . . our . . . employer?' Jane's mouth was dry all at once, and speech was difficult. 'You own this hotel?'

'We're a company.'

Bewilderedly she shook her head.

'It isn't possible,' she stammered. 'No, it – it can't be.'

'I admit the coincidence is a little incredible, but these things do happen. I couldn't see myself spending the rest of my life in the shoe business, so I looked round for something a little more interesting.' Although he proffered this information his manner was by no means friendly; on the contrary, he was now the employer – cool, aloof and rather superior. Jane looked up at him, seeing – through the confusion of her mind – a man totally different from the one she had previously known. It seemed impossible that he had ever pandered to the whims of a woman, or unhesitatingly given in whenever she had chosen to argue with him or assert her own will upon him.

'I – don't know what to say.' The murmured words came automatically, for her mind was occupied with that previous idea that Scott might have guessed at the deception being practised by her brother and herself. But surely he would have mentioned it if he had, she thought, looking into those smoky blue eyes, seeking for the expression that would reassure her completely. No, she decided, he had not guessed. A deep sigh of thankfulness and relief escaped her. At least Les's job was safe. 'You said you were on holiday,' she reminded him as the thought occurred to her. 'You're not, are you? You've come to find out for yourself whether or not we're suitable to have the management of the hotel?'

He regarded her with sudden arrogance.

'I didn't come here to snoop, if that's what you're insinuating,' he returned coldly.

She averted her head. From across the night-scented gardens the steel band music drifted, but for Jane the magic all around was no longer appreciated. She was endeavouring, through her tangled thoughts, to visualize the future and it did seem at this moment that she would be unable to remain on the island.

'You're really on holiday, then?' she managed at last.

'Partly. I came here to look for a place in which to

live.'

'You're buying a house?' She naturally thought of the lovely villas she had seen since coming to Barbados, magnificent homes, many of which had once been plantation houses owned by those who had made their fortunes by the sweat of the slaves who worked on the estates.

Scott nodded. He now lived on the island of St. Vincent, he told Jane casually, but he had recently decided to settle in Barbados. His tones remained coolly distant; his expression being one of complete indifference. Jane wanted nothing more than to escape, so that she could consider this new situation, dwell upon it and decide what she must do. Yet what could she do? she was immediately asking herself. Les had been eager to obtain a post abroad for years; at all costs she must avoid making things awkward for him. Perhaps Scott would not trouble them once he had his house on the island. After all, it wouldn't be the thing for a man in his position to keep popping in, as it were, just to see how the place was being run. Someone else would be paid to do that, surely. She would have liked to ask how long he proposed remaining at the hotel, but held back the inquiry, convinced that he would respond by making some remark that would put her well and truly in her place.

He was moving with slight impatience and she realized he was ready to leave her. Awkwardly she said good night and, turning swiftly, she went one way and Scott the other.

It was Susan who told Jane of the house which Scott was anxious to buy. Susan had telephoned the morning after Scott's arrival at the hotel and invited Jane over to Bathsheba for the afternoon. As Les made no demur Jane went eagerly, relieved to be away from Coral Gables, and the danger of meeting up with Scott again.

'Mr. Kingsley's negotiating for Driftwood House, which stands in beautiful grounds close to Paradise Beach—'

'Paradise Beach?' interrupted Jane in some dismay. 'That's only about a mile from where we are.'

'Does it matter?' Susan looked questioningly at her and Jane glanced away, avoiding her eyes. She had told Susan that Scott Kingsley was staying at Coral Gables, but that was all. She saw no reason for mentioning the fact that she and Scott had once gone about together for a short while, and certainly she would never mention that he had asked her to be his wife.

'Not really. It's just that one doesn't want one's employer living quite so close.'

'Mr. Kingsley wouldn't ever interfere. He's a charming man. We've met him only twice, but we like him enormously.' She paused, eyeing her friend curiously. 'You don't like him?' she added presently.

'I'm just indifferent,' carelessly and with the hope that Susan would leave it at that.

'We heard he was coming over and rather hoped he'd stay with us. However, he's chosen an hotel close to where the house is, which is quite understandable.' They were sitting on the balcony of the Shores' private sitting-room and down below was the swimming-pool, its blue waters stirred to a miniature storm by the playful divers and swimmers. Above, tiny wisps of cloud scudded like silver lace being gently stirred in the breeze. 'How are you liking the island?' Susan smiled as she put the question, just as if she already knew the answer.

'It's idyllic – but all these islands are, apparently.'

'That's right,' agreed Susan. 'David and I had a holiday on St. Lucia last year as you know. We loved it, but we like Barbados better, of course.' She looked towards the door and smiled as her husband entered the room behind.

'Hello, Jane,' he greeted her, coming on to the balcony. 'How's it going?'

'We love it. Les keeps on saying he has you to thank for getting him the post.'

'Nonsense.' David sat down and stretched his legs. 'I merely put forward his name when I knew the vacancy was occurring. Les did the rest himself.'

'Mr. Kingsley's staying at Coral Gables,' put in Susan. 'He arrived yesterday.'

'We'd heard he was coming. He's buying a house here,' he began to inform Jane, when Susan interrupted to say she had already mentioned this. 'It's a magnificent place,' David then continued. 'I was in it once when the owner asked us to cater for a party for him.'

'Is it an older house, or modern?' Jane looked interestedly at him and he went on to explain that Driftwood House was one of the island's most beautiful examples of the early Barbadian mansion, a typical well-cared-for plantation house with a sugar-mill in the grounds.

'It's approached by a long drive shaded by trees, and the actual gardens themselves are a dream. You see, it's been the home of an American millionaire for about twenty years and he's done wonders with it both inside and out.'

'He will have – when money was no object,' submitted Susan, while Jane, eyes pensive, tried to visualize the mansion, gaining her picture from other similar houses she had noticed when on her various rambles or when she had taken the car and gone for a drive. She knew just about were the house would be; it would have a panoramic view of the lovely coastline below and the pale gold beaches for which Barbados was famous. These beaches had been planted with coconut palms, which added majesty in addition to the exotic flavour always imparted by these particular trees.

'How does it feel being a wife?' David asked the question jocularly and only just in time did Jane prevent the frown that threatened to form on her brow.

'I'm getting used to it,' she said.

'I don't expect you cared for the idea?' from Susan, but with a hint of laughter in her voice.

'I hate deceit. But it was the only way Les could have the post. I hope there won't ever be any unpleasant repercussions.' She was thinking of Scott and wondering if she would ever approach the moment of dread when he would confront her and Les with the information that he knew they were living a lie. In such circumstances the employment must inevitably be terminated and she and her brother would return to England. It would then be most difficult for Les to get another post as hotel manager, since undoubtedly Scott would refuse to give him a testimonial.

'If you should meet someone and fall in love it would

then be rather awkward.' Susan's pretty face was creased in a frown. 'It could very well happen, you know.'

David was nodding his head in agreement. Jane shook hers.

'I don't suppose I shall meet anyone here. All the people we've met up till now are married already.'

'But you haven't met many. There are several eligible bachelors in the Yacht Club,' David told her.

'I shan't be having anything to do with that,' returned Jane with conviction. 'No, I don't think I've anything to worry about in that particular direction. It's other things that trouble me.'

'Other things?' Susan was idly drawing her fingers through her dark hair, and twisting the ends, a mannerism Jane had noticed on their very first meeting. 'What things?'

'It would be dreadful if Mr. Kingsley should discover what we'd done.'

Susan merely shrugged her shoulders and said,

'I can't see how he can.'

'I wish he wasn't settling on the island—' She stopped abruptly, not having intended to voice her thoughts aloud. 'However,' she went on resignedly, 'he is settling here, so we'll just have to hope for the best.'

'It was a pity Carolyn threw Les over. What exactly happened?' David looked interrogatingly at Jane. 'When I mentioned Les for the post at Coral Gables I was under the impression that he and Carolyn were shortly to be married. Les seemed to be settled with her, judging by his letters.'

'He admits he took too much for granted. He was

serious, but Carolyn wasn't, apparently.'

'It must have been a blow to him?'

'It was, but he never really gave up the idea of the post. I think that at first he believed he'd persuade Carolyn to marry him, so he just went ahead and attended for the interview.'

'And, later, he persuaded you to be his – er – bride.' David ended on a laughing note, but Jane's face retained its gravity. She wondered if David had considered his own position should Scott, or any other member of his company for that matter, discover the truth. He, David, had recommended Les for the post and he could never deny knowing that Jane was his sister and not his wife. It was to be hoped, for the comfort of all concerned, that the secret could be kept.

On her return to Coral Gables Jane was drawn into conversation with Mrs. Tolson, a rich South African widow who had taken a liking to Jane the moment she arrived five days previously for a three-week stay. Mrs. Tolson was small and dark with large front teeth and full, purplish lips. She wore diamonds and sapphires on her fingers and at throat; her clothes were expensive but in bad taste and on her arrival she had on a puce-coloured suit with black stripes and what Les grinningly described later as a 'distressing hat'. She walked like a man – a ponderous man, Les had said, and she always carried a gigantic bag richly embroidered with flowers. Jane's heart sank when on entering the hotel she was hailed from a chair in the lounge and had no alternative than to approach Mrs. Tolson and occupy the seat she was masterfully tapping.

'Sit down, dear child! I was just beginning to feel lonely. Where have you been all the afternoon?'

'I went over to the other side of the island to see my friends. They manage the Carib Palm Hotel at Bathsheba.'

'Bathsheba? Ah, it is a beautiful part of the island. I believe I shall have a week there before I leave, but we shall see. Now, what entertainment do we have on tonight?'

'The usual, Mrs. Tolson – limbo dancing and the steel band.'

'I thought I heard your receptionist talking to one of the porters about a fashion show?'

'That's not until Friday evening.'

'Will you have anything to fit me? It's always the silly matchstick figures you cater for in these shows!'

'I believe there are to be some clothes for the – er – fuller figure.'

'I sincerely hope so. I do need some clothes and that's for sure. And what about a barbecue? Aren't you arranging one of those for your guests?'

'I don't know, Mrs. Tolson. Perhaps we shall have one, later.'

The woman nodded.

'You haven't been here very long, I'm told?'

'Just over a week, as a matter of fact.'

'No time at all. Have you worked in hotels before?'

Jane frowned inwardly at the question.

'My br—' Appalled, she broke off, her anxious eyes darting to her companion's face. To Jane's immense relief she saw that the woman had not caught the near-mistake. 'My husband has worked in hotels all his life since leaving the training college.'

'And how long is that?'

'Twelve years. He's thirty-five.'

'So old? You must be a great deal younger than he?'

Again Jane frowned to herself.

'He's eleven years older than I.'

'Too much,' declared Mrs. Tolson emphatically. 'Men don't live as long as women in any case, and if you marry a man so much older then you're going to be left alone by the time you're fifty – just too old to get another husband.'

Jane had to laugh.

'I don't suppose I'd be wanting another husband,' she said, but the older woman was shaking her head.

'A woman always wants a husband – unless she's abnormal. I want one, I might tell you! I'm looking all the while.'

This time Jane was too diplomatic to laugh. She said, feigning interest,

'How long have you been a widow, Mrs. Tolson?'

'Five and a half years.' She gave a deep sigh. 'I do not like living alone, Mrs. Coates—' She broke off as Scott strolled across the thick carpet towards them. 'Now here,' she said *sotto voce*, 'is a man I could have my eye on were I a few years younger and he a few older. How is it that he's not married already? The women who've met him must be half asleep— Ah, Mr. Kingsley! Do join us, won't you?'

'That was my intention,' he replied courteously, and took the chair opposite to her. His eyes flickered over Jane; he noted the soft flush on her cheeks, the shading of her eyes as though she were suddenly troubled about something, and he smiled faintly to himself. He leant back comfortably and stretched his long legs. The blue eyes moved to Jane's companion and a hint of amusement entered their depths.

'What have you been doing with yourself, Mr. Kingsley?' Mrs. Tolson's thick lips curved in a smile, stretching the skin tautly. 'I did see you earlier – this morning, it was – striding along all on your own in Bridgetown. It always intrigues me to see a presentable man on his own, Mr. Kingsley. Tell me, why aren't you married? Mrs. Coates here and I have in fact just been commenting on this phenomenon.'

Starting in surprise and embarrassment, Jane would have been swift to deny making any comments about Scott, but she was prevented by his saying,

'You have?' His eyes settled on Jane's face. 'I'm flattered at being so worthy of your interest.'

Sarcastic creature! Jane's lips tightened and unconsciously she clenched her hand; Scott took notice of the angry movement and shot her a quizzical glance.

'I was just remarking to Mrs. Coates that the women who've known you must have been half asleep.'

'I don't think I understand?' The tone of icy politeness, which would instantly have disconcerted Jane, passed over Mrs. Tolson's head.

'You're a challenge to any ambitious young woman – single woman, I mean. It's rather a waste, you know, Mr. Kingsley, when a man like you remains footloose.'

The smoky blue eyes flickered to Jane's face.

'I'm afraid I'm not cut out for marriage, Mrs. Tolson,' he admitted suavely. 'As I was saying to Mrs.

Coates only yesterday – why should a man take on responsibilities when he can have all the perks without?'

Something strange stirred Jane's emotions. She found she was hating Scott's tone and the content of his words, and she wondered why she so disliked his speaking in this way.

'One day, young man, you'll meet your match!' A podgy finger topped by a scarlet nail jabbed at the arm of Mrs. Tolson's chair. 'Cleverer men than you have been caught!'

Scott's face darkened. That he was not at all pleased with Mrs. Tolson was abundantly clear. However, he retained his pleasant manner for a few minutes longer before saying to Jane,

'I wonder if I can trouble you, Mrs. Coates? There's a small matter I would like to discuss with you privately.'

'Of course.' Her heart had jerked at his request and as she rose felt strangely weak in the legs. 'Excuse me, Mrs. Tolson.'

'Come back as soon as you can, dear. I must have someone to talk to.'

'I'll try,' Jane promised, but went on to add that she would probably have to help her husband. As soon as they were out of Mrs. Tolson's hearing Jane looked anxiously into her companion's face as they crossed the lounge. 'Wh-what do you want to see me about?'

He dropped her a shrewd glance and smiled to himself.

'You sound uncommonly anxious, Jane. Is something troubling you?'

'Troubling me?' she hedged. 'No, why do you ask a

thing like that?'

'Your expression, and your tone,' he returned, an amused edge to his voice. And then he said, after a small hesitation, 'As a matter of fact, I was merely rescuing you from our friend Mrs. Tolson.'

She blinked.

'You were?' They had reached the front entrance to the hotel and Scott stopped, his gaze on the cheerful native taxi-driver who, having brought his fares to the hotel, now stood with the door open waiting for them to alight. 'That was thoughtful of you,' Jane murmured, and Scott brought his blue eyes down to her face.

'You looked so bored that I took pity on you,' he informed her quietly.

'You mean, you came over to us for that precise purpose?'

'Correct.' He seemed to lose interest suddenly, and his eyes took on an abstracted look. 'One would scarcely seek out a woman like Mrs. Tolson merely for the pleasure of her conversation.' His attention was caught again, this time by Les, who was walking very slowly towards the entrance, accompanying a very old lady who was getting along by the aid of a stick. 'Your husband appears to be a most patient man,' he observed. 'And sympathetic too. I'm inclined to think he keeps his he-man qualities just for you.' Subtle tones and fringed with a sort of mocking satire. Jane went red as she followed the direction of Scott's gaze. No one could look less masterful than her brother. Of little more than average height, he was slimly built and although his shoulders were wide they gave no impression of hidden strength. His features were benign rather than firm, his mouth gave evidence of a compassionate nature, his brown eyes rarely wore a hard expression. His ready smile appeared when he saw Scott and Jane standing there.

'Will you be all right now, Mrs. Baker?' he asked, and she nodded gratefully.

'It was nice of you to walk with me Mr. Coates,' she said. 'I do manage, you know, but I have more confidence if someone's with me. Now, I know you've promised to walk with me again tomorrow morning, but if you're busy then don't let that promise trouble you; I shall understand.' She smiled at him and then at the other two. 'I'm off to my room now, and you'll see my dinner is sent up, won't you?'

'Certainly, Mrs. Baker.'

'Isn't she a dear old lady?' Jane spoke impulsively, already having taken a liking to their oldest guest, who was eighty-seven and still travelling all over the world. 'She's a marvel! I hope I have her courage when I'm her age.'

Scott turned his head and stared at Jane with an odd expression. Her eyes were clear and bright, her mouth curved in a smile that was almost tender as she watched the old lady moving with difficulty towards the lift.

'She's a good conversationalist too,' Les was saying. 'There's never a dull moment when you're with her.'

'I haven't talked with her yet,' said Scott, 'but I must. As Jane says, she's a marvel.'

Les glanced swiftly at him; it was the first time he had heard him call his sister by her name. There was something familiar about the way he used it, so casually, as if he had a perfect right to – and yet he always referred to Les as Mr. Coates.

'It's an odd situation,' he was saying to Jane a short while later as they sat for a few moments in their private sitting-room, which was on the first floor, close to the bedroom used by Les. 'He calls you Jane, while I, as your husband, am always referred to by my surname.'

'It's because he's known me before.'

'I admit this. But now that he's our employer you'd think he'd be more formal.'

It was a strange thing, but Jane was quite unable to regard Scott as her boss.

'I expect he'd find difficulty in calling me Mrs. Coates.'

Les became thoughtful.

'When he discovered who you are – or, more correctly, who you're supposed to be – didn't he comment on the fact of your not having changed your name on your marriage?'

'Yes; I mentioned that to you when I told you all about it.'

'Did you, Jane? I'm sorry. I mustn't have been listening.' He became lost in thought again and then added, 'It's obvious that he's forgotten your brother's name was Leslie.'

She nodded.

'For which I'm overwhelmingly grateful,' she returned. 'I had a grim few minutes after suspecting that he might have guessed at the deception – and at that time I hadn't learned that he was our employer.'

'If you had it would have been ten times worse, of course.'

'Without doubt it would!'

'We're darned lucky that his memory's not all that good.'

'It could just be that I never mentioned your name. We never really became so intimate that he and I exchanged confidences, or entered into details about our respective families. I knew he had a father and a sister; he was aware I had a brother. But you know how it is sometimes – you say "my brother" or "my sister" and the actual names don't come out. I have no idea what his sister's name is.'

'He never mentioned it to you?'

'I don't think so. If he did I've forgotten it.'

'So it's the same with Scott.' Les looked at her curiously. 'What made you refuse him? You'd have done well for yourself if you'd accepted him.'

'We weren't suited.'

'I imagine he's most girls' idea of the perfect man.'

'Because he's handsome, you mean?'

'Not only that. He seems to have everything – physique, personality, strength of character.'

Strength of character . . .

'At the time,' she owned, 'I thought he was rather weak.'

Les's eyes widened.

'Weak? In what way?'

'I always managed to get my own way with him,' she replied, but with some reluctance, for it wasn't at all easy to discuss Scott with her brother. 'He gave in to me far too easily.'

Les smiled faintly.

'Like all women you wanted a man with cave-man tendencies, is that it?'

Despite herself she had to laugh.

'I didn't want a husband I could twist around my little finger.'

'You'd never have twisted Scott round your little finger,' he affirmed. 'Whatever gave you that idea?'

'It wasn't an idea, it was a fact. I had only to argue and he capitulated, immediately. I had the impression that he was afraid of incurring my displeasure.'

'He capitulated?' Les spoke disbelievingly. 'It doesn't seem possible!'

'Not now,' she readily agreed. 'He's changed considerably.'

'He must have, for I'm sure no woman would get him to capitulate now. He strikes me as a man who, when he marries, will assert his will right from the start.'

She nodded in agreement.

'I saw the change at once. It staggered me.'

A small silence and then,

'Do you think your refusal had anything to do with the change? I mean – did he know why you refused him?'

'I told him, yes. I had to,' she added hastily as Les threw her a surprised glance. 'He wanted to know why I was refusing him.'

'So your refusal could have had something to do with this change, a change which, from what I can gather, is more than a little dramatic.' Les was shaking his head even as he spoke. 'I don't believe Scott ever was weak. A man doesn't change like that. His character is what it is and that's the way it stays. It's my belief that he loved you so much that he let you have all your own way.'

She was frowning heavily. Was this the truth? Had

Scott been basically strong but so much in love that he couldn't bear to deny her anything? She bit her lip so hard that she thought she would feel blood in her mouth. She was recalling the fact that his face had remained clearly imprinted on her mind all these years; she also reflected on the circumstance of his gripping her arms when she had bumped into him last evening. Emotions had undeniably been stirred by his touch ... and so had her memory. The touch of Scott's hands had always been a most pleasant sensation. She remembered her disappointment at what at the time she had assumed to be his weakness; she had admitted to herself that if only he had asserted himself, displayed a little mastery so that she was made to realize she would not always be allowed her own way, the affair might have ended differently. Not that she would have consented to marry him right away; she was not sufficiently attracted to him at that time. But most certainly she would not have refused him with such finality. She would have suggested they continue going about together, giving her the time to discover her feelings for him.

And what would she have discovered . . .?

Jane swallowed to remove a strange dryness in her throat. It struck her only now that not once in these past four years had any other man appealed to her. Could this mean that, subconsciously, Scott occupied some important place in her heart and mind?

She spoke at last, a brooding, bewildered expression in her eyes.

'He's changed in other ways. He's cynical and sarcastic. He gave me to understand that he's found women easy and therefore marriage doesn't appeal to him. I gained the impression that he's contemptuous of all women, not merely those with whom he – er ...' Her words died away, bringing a smile to her brother's face.

'Those with whom he's amused himself?'

Jane nodded.

'Yes, that's what I meant.'

Les became lost in thought.

'Is there any possibility of your falling for him – now that his stronger qualities have been displayed?'

She shook her head, but it was an automatic gesture.

'I don't expect I shall be seeing very much of him once he's settled in his house.'

'You've not answered my question, Jane.'

She looked across at her brother, noticing the anxiety in his eyes.

'Don't worry, Les; Scott isn't interested in me any more. In any case, he's the last man to become entangled with a married woman, especially the wife of one of the company's employees.'

'I expect you're right,' thoughtfully but with a growing frown. 'He must have loved you once – and doesn't it strike you as strange that he's never married?'

'I feel that, as you suggested, my refusal did have some far-reaching effect on him, bringing about this other change I mentioned, the cynicism he displays, the sarcasm and – sort of – mockery which seems always to be with him. He probably experienced only hurt at first, when I turned down his offer of marriage, but then he must have become bitter and this led automatically to this attitude he adopts towards marriage.' She shook her head. 'He won't ever be interested in me again, Les, so there's no need for you to worry about a situation where I shall want to confess our deceit to Scott.'

'You're sure? I'd much rather tell him now, Jane, than have to do it later. If I'm to be sacked then let it be before I've put down any roots on this island.'

'You won't ever have to tell him,' she returned with conviction. 'As I've said, Scott isn't interested in me any more.'

## CHAPTER THREE

THE following morning Jane met Scott almost at the crack of dawn. Intent on seeing the sunrise from over the hills, she had risen early and was in the garden before any but the native servants in the hotel were stirring. She had naturally expected to have the entire glory of the morning to herself, and her dismay on seeing Scott emerge from the hotel brought a deep frown to her forehead.

'Hello,' was his cheerful greeting, and she managed a smile.

'Good morning, Mr. Kingsley,' she returned, and he gave a quick gust of laughter.

'I expect your husband has given you instructions to address me with respect . . . or has he *ordered* you to do so?' with mocking humour that brought the colour to her cheeks, a circumstance that appeared to increase his amusement enormously, for the blue eyes came alight, in that particular way that she remembered so well from far back in the past. 'An order would, I believe, afford you immense pleasure—' He stopped and laughed. 'Is it pleasure a woman derives from being dominated? Or excitement – or what? Do enlighten me, Jane. I'm such a fool where women are concerned . . . or is that an exaggeration? I can't remember exactly what you said. I do recall that you implied I had no strength of character.' He was mocking her, and thoroughly enjoying himself in the process. Her colour deepened as she became more and more disconcerted. This man was an enigma, someone she had never known before, nor ever would know, she thought, feeling strangely flat at the prospect of his leaving the hotel. And this was absurd, simply because she and Les would be far more comfortable once he had made his departure. 'Well, Jane, aren't you going to answer me? What emotion does a woman experience on being subjugated? I'd like to know, just for future reference.'

She gave him a speaking glance and said chokingly,

'I haven't asked for this, Scott—'

'So we're back to Scott again, are we? Watch it, Jane, or your lord and master might decide to chastise you. I think you'd better do as you're bid and treat me with respect.' She found nothing to say and he added, the light of mocking satire bringing life to those vivid blue eyes again, 'You're not all joy at the moment. Are you afraid I'll give your husband the sack?'

At that she started visibly.

'You wouldn't, Scott – Mr. Kingsley. Please say you won't take it out of my husband?'

A flicker of his eyelashes hid his expression momentarily. When presently he spoke his angular dark face was inscrutable.

'I might be lacking in strength of character and the rest,' he said crisply, 'but spite doesn't rank among my failings. Your husband seems to be most efficient and conscientious and I believe he'll be a great asset to our company.' Grave tones and the smile had gone from his eyes and mouth. He was the businessman, giving praise where praise was due.

'Thank you,' she said, breathing a sigh of relief. 'It's

nice of you to say this. My husband will be happy to know that you're satisfied with what you see here.'

A small silence followed before Scott asked why she was up so early. She wanted to see the sunrise, she told him, and his brows lifted a fraction as he pointed out that the sun had already risen.

'While we were speaking,' she agreed and, turning her head, she looked towards the hills. 'My friends will have a wonderful view,' she said mechanically. 'They'll see the sun come up from the edge of the sea.'

'Your friends . . .' He became thoughtful. 'Mr. and Mrs. Shore. I was informed by my man Spender that it was David Shore who recommended your husband for the post of manager here?'

'Yes, that's right.'

Again that thoughtful mood possessed him.

'Have you and your husband known the Shores very long?'

She became alert. If ever Scott should discover the truth then David would undoubtedly be in trouble; this Jane had already concluded and now she spoke with caution as she replied,

'We were friends in England, but we haven't seen one another for three years, until we came out here just over a week ago, that is.'

A strange expression crossed his face momentarily. He seemed amused by his reflections, but when at last he spoke she learned nothing of these thoughts.

'Are you walking, Jane – or are you returning to the hotel?' The abrupt change of conversation, while surprising, also afforded her immeasurable relief, since she surely would have floundered had Scott continued to talk about the Shores. That he should have so abruptly changed the subject did not strike her as significant at this time; later, she was to think about it . . . and learn the reason for it.

'I was intending taking a walk,' she answered, feeling awkward now and instantly regretting her words. She should have said she was returning to the hotel as then she could have escaped from him. To be with him was by far too dangerous; she was so terribly afraid of saying something which might arouse his suspicions regarding her relationship with the manager of the hotel.

'Then we'll walk together.' The firm decision held no surprise for Jane; she had known he would suggest just that. 'The beach,' he said, beginning to stroll towards it. 'I find the sea at this time of the day bewitching as a beautiful woman.' Laughter edged his words and she frowned suddenly. This man was not nearly so attractive as the Scott she had once known, she decided, immediately astounded that she should now be admitting to Scott's former attractiveness. But she could not help recalling, as she strolled along beside him on the pale gold sands, that day when he proposed to her. His voice and manner were so very gentle; he was like a young boy, not quite sure of himself yet sure of what he wanted, which was to have Jane for his wife. Twenty-six, and no experience of women. Unique, she thought, and fell to wondering how many women he'd had since that day. 'You're quiet, Jane.' His voice interrupted her reflections and she looked up into his handsome face. The lines she did not like were plain today – they branded him a cynic, a man of the world whose experience of women had bred contempt for them, and the resolution never to marry. Jane found herself swallowing a little lump in her throat. She alone was responsible for this incredible change, just as her brother had intimated . . . and she was not in the least proud of herself.

'I was thinking,' she murmured at length when, with a raising of his brows, he silently reminded her that he was waiting for her response to his words.

'About what?'

She shrugged and hoped it appeared to be a careless gesture.

'All sorts of things.'

'Non-committal, eh?' They were under a clump of coconut palms and he stopped, tall and a trifle overpowering, because of his height and his air of confidence and superiority, and because she was very conscious of the fact that he was her employer, and not the man who had wanted her for his wife. It was a strange, unreal situation in which she found herself, a situation she would not soon forget, since her pulses were racing and something quivered in the region of her heart. She remembered his touch, his kiss, his tender words just a few moments before he had asked her – with such confidence – to marry him. 'Come, Jane, tell me what was occupying your mind for so long.'

Her head was tilted and suddenly she felt his cool clean breath on her face as he bent, as if he would touch her lips with his own.

Tingling nerves and confused thoughts; a swift twist of her body that took her some distance from him; blushing cheeks and lips that trembled. Scott seemed fascinated by the picture he saw and for a long, dramatic moment of silence he stared, unmoving, at her lovely face. Then his lashes came down, masking his expression. She began to walk on again and he fell into step beside her, and after a moment or two the situation was eased and he repeated his question.

She hesitated, and then, driven by some force beyond her control, she told him candidly that she had been thinking of the change which had taken place in him since those days when they had gone about together.

'You mentioned this change before,' he reminded her, assuming a rather bored expression. 'I said I hoped it was a change for the better?'

Jane said nothing for a moment.

'You've become cynical,' she murmured, and Scott reminded her that she had also said this before.

'Is there no other change?' he added curiously, his air of boredom replaced by an expectant quality which made Jane stare at him, perplexed. For she had the odd impression that he wanted her to tell him the truth – tell him he was now arrogant and superior and full of self-assurance, in fact, to inform him that he was not in any way the man she had previously known.

'You're – different,' she stammered, quite unable to pronounce what was in her mind.

'Change usually does mean difference,' he responded with heavy sarcasm, and he watched the colour rise in her cheeks, continued to stare as she lowered her long eyelashes so that shadows fell on to her face, hiding her expression. 'What is this difference, Jane?'

She shook her head, her eyes travelling to two dark figures a long way off, running across the beach towards the silent sea. Their hands were clasped; suddenly the man jerked at the girl's arm and the couple stopped and kissed. Following the direction of her gaze, Scott smiled cynically.

'Love's young dream,' he murmured almost to himself. 'One day they'll awake, and wonder what they were about, wasting their time like that.'

His words hurt, like the prick of a thorn. She looked up at his profile, noting the taut lines, inflexible, stern, hard at this moment to the point of ruthlessness. He was still watching the couple, who were now running again, and only when they entered the water did he bring his eyes back to Jane.

'They're in love.' She spoke sharply, little knowing she was defending the couple, and in so doing was telling Scott not to be so derisive in his comments.

Scott ignored this and said,

'This difference in me on which you've twice commented – will you expand a little?'

His lips were twisted; he was mocking her, playing with her. It was incredible that he could do so . . . the 'spineless jellyfish' that she had once so foolishly termed him.

'Is it so important to you that I explain?' she asked.

He nodded.

'I'm exceedingly interested.'

Very well, she thought. He had asked for it. But she did first say,

'You're my employer—' and he instantly interrupted with,

'Don't be anxious that I shall retaliate. Haven't I said that your husband will be a valuable asset to the company?'

'Yes.' Another hesitation and then, looking away so that those keen blue eyes were avoided,

'You're – arrogant now, and hard, whereas before you were soft and – and gentle . . .'

A strange silence followed before he spoke.

'Experience, my dear,' he said. 'This changes our personalities. There's no room in this world for the man who is gentle and – er – soft, as you term it.'

Unconsciously she gave a sigh.

'You were a nicer person then—' Aghast at what she had said, she clipped off her words abruptly, but of course he had caught them and his straight brows lifted a fraction.

'You didn't consider me nice at the time,' he was swift to remind her, noting her discomfiture and obviously deriving satisfaction from it. 'You had no use for the gentle type, desiring in your husband a mastery that would keep you under, robbing you of a will of your own, reducing you to a mere shadow, a weakling who would follow where you were led. You wanted the type of man who would never allow the word obey to be dropped from the marriage vows.' He was amused now, and the blue eyes reflected this. 'Aren't I right?'

'You're distorting the whole thing, Scott – Mr.—'

'Scott will do,' he interrupted softly.

'You're exaggerating. I merely wanted a man who had strength of character.'

'And a man who is gentle is, automatically, without strength of character?'

Distractedly she made a gesture with her hand.

'You're tying me in knots.'

The protest passed over him.

'No such thing. I'm stating facts, as I saw them.'

Jane had no more to say. She wanted only to escape and her swift glance at the hotel told him this.

'Come,' he said, 'let's continue our stroll.' His voice had lightened and she found herself quite unable to keep her thoughts from wandering into forbidden zones . . . following the path that might have been had she not so impulsively formed an opinion of his character, resulting in her refusal of his offer of marriage. There would have been children by now, children brought up in this idyllic part of the world . . .

Was she in love with him, after all? The implications of such a situation hit her with stunning effect. She was 'married' and in any case, Scott was now so disenchanted with the idea of marriage that he was incapable of giving love, either to her or anyone else. She mustn't harbour the possibility that she cared – no! Forget the idea ever entered her head, or otherwise she would dwell on it and continue to do so until the day must dawn when she would face up to the truth.

'I shall have to go back,' she said at length. 'I've work to do.'

'Work?' He looked down at her. 'I thought you said you hadn't anything much to do?'

'I usually arrange flowers for the tables, and I like them to be there at breakfast time.'

'I see. Then I'll not keep you from your duties.' The employer, indifferent, cold, almost; and something contracted within her. 'I shall probably see you at breakfast time.'

She stood a moment after he had turned and strolled away, and even after she had begun to walk towards the hotel she found herself unable to resist looking back. And again she stopped. Having taken off his slacks and shirt he was standing on the edge of the water, clad in bathing trunks. So he had come out for a swim. As he went into the sea he happened to glance her way, and the colour rushed into her face as she saw in imagination the mocking curve of his mouth. She bit her lip hard, furious with herself for her weakness in standing there, watching him with such apparent interest. The man was too full of his own superiority already without her boosting it by displaying this interest.

But long after her return to Coral Gables the image of those hard, chiselled features lingered in her mind, causing her at last to admonish herself and forbid any further thought of Scott Kingsley, who was merely her employer – and nothing more.

The house stood on a small hill overlooking Paradise Beach and was approached by a long drive at the end of which pretty shade trees surrounded a fountain. Arched verandahs, shady, and cooled by the balmy breeze, looked out on to a panoramic view of the coastline below, a majestic coastline of pale yellow sands fringed with coconut palms.

Jane had been driven to the house by Scott who, a fortnight previously, having completed the purchase of Driftwood House, had told Jane she was to be his priate secretary and would therefore be working at his home. Startled, she pointed out that she had a certain amount of work to do at Coral Gables, but this was waived and the command – yes, it was a command! – had been repeated. So there was nothing for it but to do as she was told, and now she was to be shown where she would work, in close proximity to the lovely study used exclusively by Scott.

There had been something most strange about him on that day when, having happened to be bathing at the same time as Jane, he had seemed suddenly to make his decision. He knew of course the nature of her work back in England, so she could not avoid the issue by stating her inability to type and take shorthand notes. Scott had talked to Les about the appointment he was offering to Jane, and later, when Jane and her brother discussed the new and unexpected turn of events Les had looked oddly at her and said,

'It's very strange indeed. He's actually taking you away from me for the whole of the day – every day except the week-ends, of course,' he added.

'I agree that it's strange, for as far as he's concerned we're newly married, and to make me go and work for him does seem all wrong.'

Les nodded.

'With your being an old flame of his, you mean? Yes, there's something very puzzling about the whole business and I wish I could find an explanation for his action. However, you'll have to go. His word is law and that's that.'

His word is law. Jane had to smile at this, although the smile held no humour. Scott able to dictate – Scott whom she had despised because of his docility.

'Well, here we are. I hope you'll like your surroundings.' Scott's cool unemotional voice broke into her reflections and she turned her head.

'It's a beautiful house,' she responded, the eagerness in her tones escaping unbidden. 'You must be very proud to own it.'

He said nothing, and as he brought the car to a standstill she had the impression that a sudden bitterness had entered into him. But the impression died instantly and she was looking into a smiling face as he opened the car door for her to alight. The smile was unusual, for no tinge of sarcasm or cynicism was displayed in it.

'The previous owners lived in grand style,' he said at last as they entered the house through an impressive doorway flanked by fluted pillars of gleaming white coral stone. 'I'm afraid I prefer to live more simply. Parties and barbecues are all right in moderation, but the aimless round of pleasure that is in effect merely an escape from boredom is not necessary with me. I have my work, and certain other pleasures,' he added in a strangely subtle tone that caused her to stare at him and blush a little. His fine lips curved; the smoky blue eyes came alight with humour, evoking memories for Jane which stimulated emotions that had previously lain half-dormant.

'Yes,' he said after a long silent moment, 'I have other pleasures which are far more enjoyable than parties and the rest.'

Jane turned away. An innocent man she had had no time for . . . but now Scott was a rake, and she was filled with regret that the transformation had been so complete.

'Is this where I shall work?' she was asking a few minutes later when Scott had opened the door of a medium-sized room that had been fitted out with a desk and all the necessary equipment of an office. 'It's lovely!' Uninvited, she entered and crossed to the window. 'The view, Scott! I shan't be able to get any work done!' She was no longer his employee, but the spontaneous girl he had once known, and with whom he had fallen madly in love. She turned to him; he had followed her into the room and he was now by the desk, his eyes holding an unfathomable expression in their depths. She averted her head, unable somehow to hold his gaze. He drew closer; she was conscious of his nearness, of the elusive scent of soap on his hands as he spread them on asking if the equipment was to her liking. She murmured 'yes' and another silence followed, profound intense, all-enveloping. Jane had the sensation that she had entered a trap . . . no, that she had been lured into a trap, and that from this very moment she would be fighting to escape. She blinked, dazed by this absurd idea. The long lashes cast shadows on to her cheeks and as she watched something moved spasmodically in her companion's throat. The next moment he was the aloof and rather superior employer.

'Your hours will be from nine till five,' he informed her. 'As for salary – we'll discuss that later. You and your husband now have a joint salary, so obviously this will have to be separated. Your husband will have his and you yours.'

She nodded.

'When do you want me to start?'

'Monday. You can use one of the hotel taxis. Later perhaps you might like to have your own car?'

'I had thought of that.'

'You'll need some advice if you're going to buy a secondhand vehicle. I'll look it over for you when you've found something.'

Was he concerned for her safety? she wondered, strangely happy at the notion.

'Are you taking me back now?' she was asking as after leaving the room he took her along the hall with its impressive staircase, to the front verandah.

'Yes. There's nothing else to talk about at present. I shan't be here when you come on Monday morning, but you'll find several letters on your desk. Type them out while you're waiting. I'll be back about eleven o'clock.'

'You're going away for the week-end?' The question was out before she realized she had no right to ask it and she bit her lip as his brows lifted.

'That,' he said softly, 'is my business.'

'I'm sorry.'

'Your morning coffee will be brought to you by Polly – I've inherited her from the previous owners, along with most of the other servants. Polly will make your coffee at whatever time you require it.'

'Thank you,' said Jane, feeling awkward now that Scott's manner had become brisk and business-like.

'Is there anything you would care to ask me?'

She shook her head.

'I can't think of anything at the moment.'

'In that case I'll take you back to Coral Gables.'

He drove the car in a circle before getting back on to the drive, and Jane gasped inwardly at the spectacle she had of the gardens. Exotic flowers abounded, exuding sweet perfumes. Flames of crimson marked the lovely flamboyant tree; the frangipanis glowed, pink and white, their heady fragrance mingling deliciously with that of the other tropical flowers. The weeping willow type branches of the red bottle-brush tree were ablaze with scarlet tassels; golden shower and cape myrtle, oleanders and flame of the forest flowered beside the mahoganies and tamarinds and the graceful casuarinas.

'Is that forest yours?' she asked when presently all this splendour was left behind and they were making their exit through the gateway.

'Forest?' in some amusement. 'It's merely a wood. Yes, it goes with the house. I believe many monkeys have made it their home.'

'Monkeys? How delightful! I haven't seen one yet.'

'No? They're here. You'll occasionally see them running across the road over on the eastern part of the island. I've seen them myself.'

'I've seen a mongoose dashing across, but not a monkey.'

'Then you'll have to wander in these woods; you're bound to see them there.'

'The island used to be covered with dense forests,' she murmured conversationally after a while.

'That's so, but deforestation was necessary for the growing of the sugar cane. You'll have noticed that it grows in profusion here in Barbados?'

'Yes, I have. You seem to go through one endless plantation as you travel to the east coast. No wonder it's called the sugar island.'

'That is one name for it . . .' A pause and then, 'There's another, much more romantic name. Have you not heard it?'

'No, I haven't.'

'Isle of the purple moonflower,' he told her. 'Rather pretty, don't you think?'

Was there an edge of sarcasm to his tone? She somehow felt that his cynicism was very much to the fore.

'Pretty indeed and as you say, romantic.' She said that just to note his reaction, but he was concentrating on his driving and no comment was forthcoming. And for the rest of the short journey he remained silent, thoughtfully so. She wondered at his thoughts . . . and she wondered where he was intending to spend the coming week-end . . .

## CHAPTER FOUR

It was a month since Jane had come to work as secretary to Scott. It had been the most difficult period she had ever known. Scott had turned out to be the most severe and fault-finding taskmaster, his own competence, like his tongue at times, being a lash which stung intolerably.

'I can't go on,' she once told Les, but instantly regretted her words, so concerned did he become.

'Is he so difficult to work with?'

'To work for,' she corrected. 'Scott never for a moment allows me to forget that he's my boss.'

'I can't think why he should be like this. David and Susan like him enormously, as you know. He appears to be kindness itself to me as well.' A pause, as he glanced curiously at her. 'It must be you,' he declared at length, and she nodded understandingly.

'He's getting his own back.' And yet it was not feasible, since such mean and petty conduct was totally at variance with the fineness of his character.

'If you want to throw the whole thing in, Jane, please don't consider me. I'm to blame for the deception, since you never wanted it, so I'll take the consequences. Leave if you wish, and we'll go back to England.'

Without hesitation she shook her head.

'You love it here, and we're staying.'

Les was clearly relieved and Jane knew she could never bring herself to act in a way that would result in his losing his job. She must endure all Scott gave her, and hope that he would mellow with time. She certainly tried hard to do things right, but he seemed intent on finding fault and she gained the impression that his intention was to keep her constantly aware of his superiority over her, aware that he was her boss and his orders were to be carried out to the letter. Sometimes, though, she would think she glimpsed a vision of the man she had known before – the gentle, kindly man, the one whom, at that time, she had not found attractive enough to marry. And now . . . What a perverse creature woman was! Now, she would have done anything to hear the tender words, see that soft light enter the deep-set blue eyes. What did her longings mean? Jane thrust away the persisting light that as yet was no more than a glimmer, like dawn's first gentle ray. But at the back of her mind she was terribly afraid, and often recently she would recall that sensation of having been lured into a trap.

'Jane!' The word was rapped out and she jumped visibly. She was sitting at her typewriter, but her thoughts occupied her completely and she had not even heard Scott's entry into her room. 'I expected that report long ago. What have you been doing?'

'I'm sorry. I've almost finished it.'

He looked sternly at her, noting her rising colour.

'Bring it to me immediately it's finished. I want it in the post this afternoon.' And with that he strode out, pulling the door to behind him.

'I'm sorry I was a long time.' The second apology accompanied the handing over of the report some twenty minutes later. 'I hope you'll find it all right.'

Scott took it from her, his eyes on her face.

'I hope so too. As if it isn't all right it'll not catch the post.' A threat in the tones and in his sharpened expression. Jane said a little prayer, which was destined to be answered, the report being such that Scott was unable to find the slightest flaw in it.

'What shall I do then?' she asked when, having read it over again, Scott told her to get it ready for mailing.

'You can go,' he answered, glancing at his watch. 'And tomorrow you can have the day off; I'm going away and won't be back until Monday.'

'Thank you.' She left his study, aware of a strange feeling of dejection. It was an absurd truth that although at times her life as Scott's secretary was almost unbearable, she took no pleasure at all in these Fridays off which he gave her. This was the third time it had happened. She supposed she hated the idea that had become firmly fixed in her mind – the idea that Scott had a girl-friend in St. Vincent, where he used to live and where he spent these week-ends. He had mentioned St. Vincent on the telephone one day when he happened to be talking to someone, and although Jane, having knocked, and entered his room, had immediately left it again, she had heard enough to establish the fact that he went to St. Vincent for these week-end breaks from business matters. Why she should assume he had a girl-friend she was not sure, but he *had* made those remarks about having 'other pleasures' and she supposed this was sufficient to plant the first germ of suspicion in her mind.

Was she in love with him? she asked herself again, just as she had on that morning when they had strolled together on the private beach of the Coral Gables

Hotel. And, as on that occasion, she shirked the answer, thinking of the implications and remembering that Scott could never return her love even were he to learn that she was free. Yet that glimmer of light, shining in her subconscious, daily became brighter, more illuminating. This she freely owned as time passed. And when her first couple of months as Scott's secretary had gone by she was unable any longer to mask the light by evasion. She was irrevocably in love with him; and the flat, hopeless feeling that settled on her was made all the more bitter by the knowledge that he could have been hers, four years ago.

But not now. He had no interest whatsoever in her as a woman, and his indifference stabbed like the sharp point of a sword. The result of her own knowledge was a constraint in her manner with him and gradually their relationship deteriorated to such an extent that she felt sure he would soon dispense with her services as secretary and let her resume her duties at the hotel. But he carried on, and she once again felt sure he intended to make her feel her position as his employee.

It was the night before the barbecue arranged by Les that Scott came to Coral Gables and dined there, with a tall dark girl who, to Jane's critical eyes, was both artificial and conceited. Introducing her as Alma Bonsall, Scott seemed inordinately interested in Jane's reaction. With dignity she overrode the ordeal, but the pain went deep within her. She was jealous – primitively so. She hated the girl from the moment of setting eyes on her as the entered the dining-room, one elegantly-manicured hand resting on the sleeve of her escort's white dinner jacket. Her slender figure was clad in a clinging gown of silver lamé, a gown which revealed just about as much as decency permitted. Her hair, almost black and swept away from her face to form a pleat at the side of her head, was lustrous and thick, and as Jane's imagination broke bounds she saw this abundance of silken tresses falling all about the girl's elegant shoulders . . . saw Scott's hands running through it with typical male enjoyment. Yes, she hated the girl, but managed to retain an indifferent front.

'Will you find us a secluded corner, Jane?' The request, spoken in an over-crisp tone, brought from her a darkened glance and a slight smile touched Scott's mouth. He appeared rather satisfied with himself about something, she thought, politely asking him to follow her.

'This is the best we can do,' she told him coolly. 'Had you rung to make a reservation we could have found you a table over there . . . among the palms.'

'This will do nicely, thanks.' He pulled out a chair for Alma, whose gaze was interestedly fixed on Jane.

For a fleeting second Jane met the girl's supercilious eyes and then, to Scott,

'I'll see that you have a menu, Scott, and the wine list.'

'Scott,' she heard Alma say as she left the table. 'But I thought you said she was an employee of yours . . .?' That was all Jane heard, but it was enough to make her grind her teeth. The tone of the girl! But perhaps she had caught the superiority from Scott, thought Jane spitefully.

'Is anything wrong?' Les asked the question immediately he and Jane were seated at their table. A Captain Reeves and his wife were to join them, but for the moment they were alone. 'You look furious about something.'

She had not realized her feelings were so transparently revealed and at her brother's words she brought forth a smile.

'You're imagining things, Les,' she answered carelessly. 'What would I be furious for?'

He shrugged.

'I don't know. You just didn't seem yourself, I thought.' His eyes strayed to the table by the wall, lit by one small candle in a vase shaped like a broad-petalled flower. 'Scott's got himself a bundle of glamour and no mistake,' he commented after a pause. 'I wonder if she's his steady?'

'Of course she isn't!' snapped Jane, and her brother's eyes opened wide.

'So . . .'

She coloured.

'So – what?'

'You don't care for his having female company, I take it?'

'I don't give a toss about his company! Scott Kingsley means nothing to me.'

Les's eyes flickered.

'I hope you're sure, Jane,' he said at length in anxious tones.

'Certainly I'm sure.' Her voice was more moderated now and although her brother looked searchingly at her he made no further comment, and in any case, they were very soon joined by Captain and Mrs. Reeves and from then on the conversation became light and entertaining.

The Captain danced with Jane. He was tall and

distinguished with bushy grey hair and a large moustache. Catching Scott's gaze momentarily as he danced with his glamorous partner, Jane perceived that sardonic expression in his eyes and immediately glanced away. What was he trying to do to her? she could not help wondering. She had suspected him of retaliation for what she had long since done to him, then decided such an action was too petty for a man like Scott. And yet it would certainly seem that he had something in mind, and the more Jane thought of this the stronger grew her conviction.

As she had half expected, the moment arrived when he asked her to dance. She rose stiffly, and treated him to a cool and forced little smile. He said, once they were away from her table,

'You don't seem happy this evening, Jane. Is something the matter?'

Her mouth went tight; he saw it and gazed inquiringly at her.

'I'm perfectly all right, thank you.'

'Angry, obviously.' The blue eyes twinkled with taunting amusement. Jane felt she could have enjoyed saying something to wipe that expression from his face, but unfortunately nothing appropriate occurred to her.

'You shouldn't have left your friend,' she said.

'I didn't. I should have thought you'd be more observant; Alma has met an old flame of hers and he's dancing with her now—' Deliberately Scott swung Jane right round to that the girl and her partner were visible. 'Just so you'll know that whatever else I lack my manners at least leave nothing to be desired.'

'Sarcasm,' she could not help retorting, 'is the lowest

form of wit!'

'And clichés the instruments of the unimaginative,' was his swift riposte, and Jane flushed.

'You really shouldn't try to spar with me,' he added when she remained silent, endeavouring to get over her discomfiture. 'You're not sufficiently experienced in the art.'

'How pompous you are! And so very sure of yourself!'

'Jane,' he murmured softly, 'do try to remember that I'm your boss.'

'Employer!'

Scott laughed.

'You're in a very bad temper tonight. I shall cure you later.'

'You—? At his subtle warning she threw him a startled glance, leaning away as she did so, and in order to prevent her from bumping into someone Scott jerked her back. She trod on his toe, which did nothing for her dignity, and in addition he found herself so close to him that it seemed every muscle in his hard body was pressed against her. Embarrassed, she endeavoured to draw apart, but he kept her where she was.

'Well, Jane,' he said close to her ear, 'you were about to make some comment . . .?'

She swallowed, and to her extreme annoyance she trod on his toe again.

'Please let me go,' she almost snapped. 'What are you supposed to be doing?'

'Dancing with you – but you appear to have lost your skill all at once.' Mocking satire in his tones – and that detestable gleam in his eyes. Jane felt her fury straining at the bonds. She could not trust herself to speak, lest she raised her voice, and so she followed where he led and cautiously retained a silence. 'Have you lost your tongue as well?' came the infuriating question after a while, and now she did manage to draw herself from that close embrace.

'Tell me,' she said, trying to be patient, 'are you enjoying all these taunting comments you make?'

He only laughed and said,

'Would you be flattered if I told you I enjoy every moment I spend in your company?'

Her heart leapt . . . then sank again. The man was playing with her; this she must remember, always.

'I wouldn't believe you,' she said.

'I'm desolated.' His blue eyes rested on her upturned face, narrowed and faintly mocking.

'You seem to forget I'm married.' This would put a stop to it all, she decided, but she was wrong.

'Married . . .' pensively and with the most odd inflection. 'Ah, yes; I do admit that for the moment I'd quite forgotten. You know,' he added contemplatively, 'you're not at all like a married woman.' He received a startled glance and the narrowed eyes became mere slits. 'I remember my sister, when she was first married. She used to look at her husband with a sort of worshipful gaze, and she would impulsively push her arm into his in a little affectionate gesture. She called him darling no matter who was there—' Scott broke off and shrugged. 'Times have changed, I suppose, and people don't now reveal their feelings. Nevertheless, I'm sure you must be very much in love—' Again he broke off, and this time she had the extraordinary impression that he was suppressing laughter. What an enigmatical creature he was! Jane did wish she could understand him. 'Yes,' he continued presently, 'very much in love – as is your husband, although he doesn't show it either.'

'It would hardly be the thing for us to kiss and cuddle in public,' she said defensively, and Scott's laugh actually rang out.

'You're so right,' he agreed and, swinging her round, he reached her table just as the music stopped. 'Thank you, Jane. I shall see you later . . . remember?' His brows were raised, his lips twitching. 'I promised to do something to restore your good humour,' he added in a whisper, and then he was gone to join his beautiful companion.

What did he mean? Jane frowned inwardly, and found her appetite was fast losing its keenness.

True to his word he came to her, long after dinner, when the guests were outside on the terrace, listening to the calypso singers and the steel band. Muted illumination and perfumed air added to the glamour of the tropical scene. The night, balmy and starlit, was one of sheer enchantment such as can be found only in the islands of the Caribbean. Jane sat with her brother, the Captain and his wife having gone for a stroll along the beach.

'Here comes Scott,' said Les, and Jane glanced around to see where Alma was.

'Mr. Coates,' said Scott politely, 'would you mind very much if I took your wife off for a few minutes?'

'Of course not,' with an eagerness that brought a darkling frown from his sister. 'Well,' he amended at once, 'er – where are you taking her?' Was this all right? he seemed to be saying to his irate sister who, it would appear, now had not the patience even to look at him.

'Oh, only for a stroll.'

'Fine—' Les stopped. Jane glanced at Scott, whose face was an unreadable mask. 'If it's all right with my – my wife.'

Jane drew a deep breath. Really, Les would be giving the whole show away one of these days! To agree so eagerly to another man's taking her off. And what of Scott? His attitude was puzzling in the extreme; Jane thought that at least he would display a little more tact. He didn't seem to think there was anything at all wrong with asking her 'husband' if he could take her for a stroll.

'Is it all right with you?' inquired Scott, and as she seemed to have no alternative she said yes and rose from her chair.

'What happened to Alma?' she asked as they left the table, Scott's hand cupping her elbow in a possessive and masterful kind of way.

'Alas, she deserted me for another.'

Jane stopped and turned.

'There's something I don't understand,' she said, eyeing him suspiciously. 'If Alma's your – your girl-friend then why aren't you with her? Don't you mind that she's with this old flame of hers?'

'Mind? No, why should I? This is a permissive society, remember. We just move around, as it were, from one to another.'

She swallowed hard, conscious of pain and regret – and contrition because she herself had brought about this change in him. She recalled that she had not wanted an inexperienced man for a husband; she had told herself that Scott should have learned all about women before asking one to marry him. Well, it would seem that he had learned all about them, and he was a different man because of it – cynical, sarcastic, contemptuous of her sex. He accepted that it was permissible for his girl-friend to have another man, so obviously he had no ideals left. But she herself did have ideals; she could never accept it as right that people should move around, as Scott had so casually said, from one to another.

'Where are we going?' she asked as Scott began to walk on again.

'Into the remote fastnesses of the grounds,' he answered teasingly. 'Into the darkness and the privacy of the tropical garden, where we'll find a quiet spot and – er – talk.'

She stopped again, but Scott gripped her arm tightly and she was propelled towards the darkness, and the loneliness of the grounds, away from the lights and music and the laughing, chattering guests who were staying at Coral Gables.

'I don't want to – to talk,' she said, trying once more to stop in her tracks.

'Then we won't talk.' His grip tightened and she almost cried out. This man was *not* the Scott she had known. He couldn't possibly be! No one could change so much as this— 'We'll make love instead!' And before she could grasp his intention she was in his arms, and his mouth forced itself against hers, pressing hard until she felt her lips must surely be bruised. She struggled, naturally, but to no avail. Tears stung her eyes as the previous gentleness of Scott's kisses came back to her. Tender he had been, and his arms about her were a mere caress. But now he was the demanding master, in full command of the situation, determined to make her aware of his strength.

'Let me go!' she cried when at last his lips moved to her neck and then lower to where he was finding the curve partly revealed by the low V of her neckline. 'Let me go, I say! You're forgetting again that I'm married!'

He gave a short crisp laugh and took her chin in his hand, forcing it up.

'Married . . . and are you in love?'

'Of – of course—'

'Liar! And because you're not in love there's no reason why we shouldn't enjoy ourselves. Your husband will never know—'

'You must be mad! That – that *person*, Alma, might be that sort, but I am not!' Her eyes blazed; she stamped her foot hard on the ground. 'If you don't let me go I shall scream!'

'You'll not scream,' he returned with confidence. 'Kiss me again—'

'Again?' she quivered. 'I haven't kissed you at all yet!'

'Ah, but you have, many times. Have the past four years been so long that your memory's dulled?'

'Let me go,' she pleaded, spent now and breathless. Her body felt crushed, so strong was his hold on her. 'Take me back, Scott, please.'

'Do you really want to go back?' His low voice mocked; it was clear that he expected her to capitulate and she felt choked with disgust. The man was hateful!

'Most certainly I want to go back.'

His lips found hers again, cruel and fierce.

'Sure?' he whispered in a moment, and this time she

found she could not answer. For his kiss had stirred her senses, and her emotions; his arms about her, strong and ruthless in their hold, had set her pulses racing. She felt as if all her own strength was giving way under the domination of his. Was this what she desired, after all? Was this the mastery she had decided she required in the man she would eventually marry? No, she told herself fiercely . . . and yet the next moment she was as putty in his embrace, responding to his kisses and the pressure of his lean lithe body against hers. The wild throbbing of her heart was threatening to choke her when at last sanity returned and she began to struggle in his arms. But how useless it was to expend her last remaining strength!

'You might just as well give in,' he said as if reading her thoughts. 'I'm the master, Jane, and you shall succumb to my will.' Inexorable tones, and emphasized. Jane felt defeated under the impression that he meant to prove to her that he was after all strong enough to conquer her.

'You've changed so much, Scott,' was all she could find to say when he at last afforded her the opportunity to speak.

'That again?' Not the slightest measure of contrition, not the least flicker of apology or regret in his eyes as they considered her in the faint light afforded by the stars shining down from a clear Caribbean sky. 'Of course I've changed. And for the better, I hope. Didn't you enjoy being mastered?'

Too disgusted to speak, Jane fell into a brooding silence. And after a short while she saw his face slowly soften and a faint smile touch the hard outline of his mouth. He reminded her quietly that she had not answered his question and she managed to say,

'No, I didn't enjoy being – being mastered.'

'Jane . . . you little liar,' he returned softly, and he touched her forehead with gentle fingers, pushing them through her hair for a moment before letting the palm of his hand come to rest on her clear wide brow. 'You were afraid, I know, but deep down you enjoyed it. No,' he said when she would have interrupted him, 'don't lie again. It's not like you to be dishonest.'

She caught her lip between her teeth. This sudden gentleness, taking her by surprise after the way he had treated her, seemed to deprive her of speech. All she knew was that this was a moment of sweet contentment; Scott was the man she had known before and not the cynic he had turned out to be. But quite suddenly she remembered she was supposed to be married and with a little inward gasp she wondered just what Scott was thinking about her. Did he conclude that she too was one of those who went from one to another? The idea hurt excruciatingly and brought forth the rushing reminder that she had a husband.

'You – we shouldn't . . .' she added, and then tailed off, puzzled by his expression.

'Feeling guilty?' The gentle tone was replaced by that of the cynic and Jane felt her whole body sag. What was this man doing to her? 'My dear Jane, isn't it a little late for regrets and self-recrimination? You and I shall find pleasure together; your husband will find pleasure with another woman. That's how it is today, so let us be in the fashion and take what life has to offer.'

She stared up into his face, her mouth quivering and a dampness settling on her brow where his hand had been. She knew for sure that the interlude of gentleness was now regretted by Scott. It was part of his old self that he wanted to cast off, for ever. Tears stung her eyes; she was only now fully conscious of what she had lost. The old gentle Scott Kingsley had been a rare product in this present-day world, a man in a million.

And she had let him go.

'Will you take me back now?' she begged, in a hopeless, trembling tone. 'Please, Scott.'

'I said I'd force you to succumb to my will,' he reminded her, a curious inflection in his voice and an equally curious expression in his eyes as he looked searchingly into hers.

'I hope you didn't mean it.'

'Shan't we find pleasure together?'

She frowned and shook her head.

'It's absurd even to suggest such a thing.'

'Because you're married?' he said, the strange inflection returning to his voice.

'Not only that. I'm not the sort of girl you assume me to be.'

A small pause and then, with taunting satire,

'You're an old-fashioned girl? Is that what you're telling me?'

Her misted eyes were raised to his.

'You probably don't believe me, because you're so cynical and contemptuous of women, but I am an old-fashioned girl, as you like to term it.'

His underlip rolled in a sneer.

'There aren't any old-fashioned girls left, Jane.'

She said unhappily,

'Do you enjoy being like this – so lacking in

ideals?'

The blue eyes glittered.

'I once said that experience breeds cynicism; it also strips a man of his ideals.'

'It seems to me that you've met the wrong types of women.'

'Basically, there's only one type.'

'That's nonsense!'

'All right,' he conceded, 'there are one or two types – but they're all branches of the same tree. You have the good-time woman whose object it is to get rich quick; you have the one who prefers to legalize her wantonness, so she casts her net wide to find a rich husband; then you have the most honest of the three – the one who owns that sex is her business, her means of livelihood—'

'Stop!' she cried. 'I hate you when you talk like this!'

'Hate?' with a raising of his brows. 'Do you have emotions strong enough for hate? Remember, my dear,' he continued softly, 'that you're married. Any strong emotions should be kept for your husband.'

She looked at him.

'And yet, only a few moments ago, you suggested we – we enjoy ourselves with one another.' That was difficult to say, but once she had begun she did not see how she could cut off her words.

'Do we need to have strong emotions for that? After all, it would only be a calculated situation—'

'Stop it!' she flashed again, clenching her fists. 'I won't listen! Take me back, at once!'

He shrugged.

'Obviously you're not in the right mood for making

love, so back we shall go.' But he pulled her close against him and bent to kiss her, and this time there was a touch of gentleness mingling with the mastery, and there was a touch of persuasion as well, which she resisted, but with difficulty. 'Probably another time,' he murmured, his lips caressing her face. 'Yes, I'm sure your mood will change.'

'It never will!' She again remembered her 'husband' and added, 'You keep on forgetting I'm married.'

That short crisp laugh rang out again.

'We both keep on forgetting you're married.'

Startled by his tone, she stared at him, wide-eyed and fearful.

'Scott,' she began quiveringly. And she went no further because he interrupted her, speaking slowly and with a hint of amusement in his voice,

'Yes, Jane, I know. I'm not quite without intelligence; Les . . .' The straight brows were raised, the blue eyes alight. 'Need I continue? You're blushing already – and it's not one of your pretty blushes, but the blush of shame. I don't want to increase your embarrassment—'

'How long have you known?' He had released her altogether and she stepped back, away from him.

'Why, from the first, of course. You made a few slips – like hesitating before saying "husband", but of course it was the room which set me thinking, even before you and I met that first day.'

'The room?'

'I picked up the book from the desk just after my arrival. The receptionist had gone off for the moment and there was no one there. I noticed that room seventeen, which was next to that given to the manager and his wife, had not been occupied by any guest for the past week. Now, the hotel was supposed to be full. I was given the one and only available room. As I was coming from the hotel a short while later I heard the receptionist turn a single man away . . . and yet room seventeen was unoccupied – or so it would appear, by the entries in the book. I was puzzled, but before I had time to seek out the manager I met you—' Scott spread his hands. 'It was all explained. You're not very clever, Jane. Someone, some time, was going to discover that room seventeen was never given over to a guest. My man Sanders comes round periodically and he'd have noted the odd circumstance.'

Jane had gone white while he was speaking, and now she placed a trembling hand unconsciously on Scott's sleeve.

'Please . . . you won't – won't dismiss my brother?'

He shook his head thoughtfully.

'Not if you treat me with the respect due to me, and if you do as you're told. As I said, we should find pleasure with one another.'

The colour returned to her cheeks.

'You're despicable!'

A long brown forefinger was wagged close to her face.

'That respect I mentioned. Remember it – or else!'

## CHAPTER FIVE

For several hours after going to bed Jane lay awake. The incredible change in Scott's character occupied her thoughts for a long while, and then she found herself thinking about Alma and Scott's casual acceptance of the fact that she had someone else as well as him. She went over in detail the scene of ardour, blushing in the dark on recalling the things Scott had said to her. And lastly she dwelt on his assertion that they would find pleasure with one another. He had repeated this just before leaving her, and although she had turned on him angrily he had merely laughed and prophesied that she would come to a different frame of mind eventually. The final words had been,

'And don't tell your brother that I know of the deception. It doesn't serve my purpose for him to be enlightened. Understand?'

'But—'

'Understand?'

She had nodded and left him, admitting after a short while that it was best for her brother to remain in ignorance, at least for the present. Jane knew him well, and although he had daringly entered into the deception, she was well aware that a disclosure of his deceit would weigh so heavily upon him that without doubt he would throw up his job. Did Scott also suspect this? He had said a strange thing – that it did not serve his purpose for Les to be told that his deception was known by his employer. Scott had previously stated that Les would prove to be an asset to the company, so it did seem that in this lay the explanation for his refusing to allow Jane to disclose the truth to her brother.

The first light of dawn was filtering through the curtains when at last she dozed. But it was a fitful sleep into which she eventually fell and on meeting her brother at the breakfast table she was not surprised when he questioned her, his good-natured face anxious and his eyes dark with concern.

'No,' she replied, 'there's nothing wrong with me. I just didn't sleep very well, that's all.'

'Scott,' he began, 'he was with you a very long time. His girl-friend came back and seemed to be looking for him.'

'We were in the garden, talking.' Jane fidgeted with her toast, spreading the butter without actually knowing what she was doing.

'Talking?'

'Just chatting,' she replied carelessly.

'Jane . . . you're not – I mean, you and he—?'

'Les, I told you that Scott has no interest in me any more.' She managed to inject a lightness into her voice, but Les said anxiously,

'You yourself? How do *you* feel about *him*?'

She shrugged.

'How does one usually feel about an old flame? We parted because we weren't suited. It wasn't as if we were engaged or anything serious like that.'

'But he did ask you to marry him. I can't imagine Scott Kingsley going that far unless he was sure of what he was doing. And he's never married. Isn't that significant?'

'Not particularly. He prefers to have a good time, like many other men.'

'You're sure you're happy about this business – about you and me being married, I mean?'

'I'm not happy,' she admitted. 'You knew from the first that I hated the deception, but I agreed to it finally and I'm willing to abide by my decision.'

'If you were able to tell Scott you were free it might make a difference to your life. To be the wife of a man like him would appeal to a great many women.'

Jane sighed inwardly. It was difficult to obey Scott's injunction not to tell Les that he, Scott, was aware of the deception.

'Scott would never want to marry me, so there's no need for you to be anxious, Les. And now, please let the matter drop. There are other more important things to discuss. Is everything arranged for the barbecue tonight?'

'Almost. But of course I shall be busy all day. Will Scott be coming, do you think?'

'I shouldn't be surprised.'

'Then it must be perfect. I'm hoping great things might come out of this job, Jane,' he confided suddenly, his voice lightening and an eagerness entering his eyes. 'Scott seems very taken with what I've already done. He's remarked on several changes I've made, so he's obviously taking notice. The company have much larger hotels than this and I'd love to manage a really grand place.'

Jane said nothing. It was just as she had thought. The secret must be kept, for otherwise her brother's whole future could be jeopardized.

Half an hour later she was on her way to Driftwood

House, her thoughts darting about in all directions but always returning to the moment when she would come face to face with her employer. How would he react to seeing her, in the cold light of the morning? She herself must surely colour, since the whole scene would rise before her, the scene in the dark garden of Coral Gables, when Scott had held her in his arms and forced his kisses on her. That she would go through the most embarrassing few moments of her life there was no doubt at all.

Just as she suspected, Scott greeted her with that look of sardonic amusement, enjoying her discomfiture, his eyes never leaving her flushed face.

'Well, how are we this morning?'

'I'm very well, thank you.'

'You didn't sleep well, obviously,' he observed after a while. 'Thinking of me?'

She sent him a speaking glance and said coldly,

'I have other more interesting things to think about.'

He laughed.

'Such as?'

Jane was in his study; she asked what she must do.

'You said there was a report to type,' she reminded him.

His eyes narrowed.

'Don't adopt that attitude with me,' he recommended softly. 'You work for me; I've warned you to remember this.'

Jane averted her head.

'I'd like to keep the whole thing on a business footing,' she said at length. 'As you say, I work for you, as your secretary, and our relationship should begin and end with this.'

'A business footing, eh?' Scott became thoughtful. There was an enigmatical quality about him that she had noticed before and once again she wished for nothing so much as to be able to understand him. 'Perhaps you're right, Jane. We'll see.' And he instantly became brisk, giving her her orders for the day. She said automatically,

'Shall I type the report first?' and just as automatically she was at the door, opening it and passing through, her footsteps silent on the thick carpet. The door closed and she moved along the corridor to her own room where she dropped the report on her desk and sat down at the typewriter. Slowly she removed the cover, aware of tears on her lashes. A business footing ... The last thing she wanted, yet she had requested it. And Scott had half agreed, appearing indifferent, as though the matter were no longer of any real interest to him. Last night, though, he had been quite emphatic about their finding pleasure with one another, as he had put it. Not like him to switch about, she mused, eyes narrowing. The game he was obviously playing with her was affording him some amusement, no doubt, but if he had any plans up his sleeve for her eventual surrender then he could think again! Her ideals meant a lot to her and she had no intention of allowing Scott or any other man to rob her of them.

'I'll never be his *woman*,' she whispered fiercely, 'no matter how I feel about him!'

She took the report, neatly typed, back to Scott later in the day. Their eyes met briefly as she placed it on his desk; taking it up, he turned back the cover and for a space he looked at the first page in frowning contemplation. Jane felt a quickening of her pulse as she watched his changing expression while he flicked over the pages.

'You've missed something out,' he told her, his voice over-crisp. 'On the first page.' Having returned to it he began perusing it again. 'Yes, and now all the page numbers will be wrong.'

'I've missed something out?' Jane caught up her lower lip in vexation; she had known all the morning that her mind had not really been on her work, but she would not have thought she had made a mistake like this. 'I'll go and fetch your original copy.'

The report was tossed at her and she picked it up.

'It seems to me that a whole page of my copy is missing.'

Jane was reading through the first page of her own copy.

'It doesn't read as though there's anything missing—'

'Jane!' he interrupted sharply, '*I* say there's something missing! Don't stand there arguing; go and bring my copy!'

'Yes.' Leaving the report on his desk, she left the room, stinging from the anger in his voice. He had spoken sharply to her before this, very sharply on occasions, but never had she been so hurt by his manner as she was today.

'You're right,' she was saying a few minutes later. 'I've missed out a full page.'

Scott drew an impatient breath.

'You'll have to do the whole thing again.'

She refrained from argument, realizing at once that she would receive the full lash of his tongue were she to protest, as she had protested once before. But she had no intention of re-typing the whole; she could quite easily rub out the numbers and re-number each page. This she did, after inserting the extra page. But she had reckoned without her employer's keen eyesight and immediately she presented the report she regretted her disobedience. His eyes came up, narrowed and stern.

'I thought I told you to re-type all of this.' He tapped it with his finger. 'Perhaps you'll explain why you haven't done as I ordered?'

'It – it seemed unnecessary to do it all again. The numbers are neatly done—' The crash of his hand on the desk cut her short and she actually jumped. 'I'm sorry . . .'

'When I give instructions I expect them to be carried out.' The report was actually flung across the desk; it would have slid on to the floor had not Jane stepped forward to catch it. 'Do it again!' The command was rapped out with unbelievable imperiousness.

'Today?' Automatically she glanced at the clock, an action which brought a glint to the hard blue eyes.

'Yes,' said Scott in a very soft tone, a tone far more deadly than the one he had just used. 'Today.'

Jane opened her mouth to protest, aware that she would have to put in at least two hours' overtime, and Les would be needing her, especially this evening, when they were having the barbecue. But she very soon decided against voicing her protest. Scott's expression was quite enough to still her tongue.

It was ridiculous for him to demand a whole re-typing, she thought, her anger rising as she looked at him. But she was under no illusion as to the reason for the order. Once again he was letting her see that he was the boss, and she merely his employee. She had asked for it, of course, requesting as she had that their relationship remain on a business footing. It was not only that, though; Scott, she now had to accept, was in fact getting his own back for what she had done to him four years ago. Out of character it might be, but it was there, for what other reason could he have for treating her in this way?

She was very tired when at last she finished her work. Scott was not in his study and she left the report on his desk and went home to Coral Gables. Les had rung through to Driftwood house earlier and she had told him she would be working late.

'I think it was rather mean of Scott,' Les said with a frown on noting how tired she looked. 'You should have told him you hadn't slept very well last night and he might then have let you do the work tomorrow.'

Jane said nothing; Scott had guessed that she hadn't slept, but the knowledge had not made any difference.

'I'm sorry I wasn't here to help you. I hope it's all in order?'

Les nodded.

'Yes. I have a marvellous staff here.'

'I suppose I'd better get ready,' she said with a sigh. She would far rather have gone to bed, but she had promised Les she would wander about among the guests, giving special attention to those old people who were alone. There seemed to be so many of them, mainly women, and they looked forward to Jane's interest in them, and her conversation. 'I'll see you later.' She smiled at her brother and went up to her room. Life was becoming more and more difficult, and although she was glad for her brother's sake that they were here, she did wonder just how long she could tolerate Scott's strange moods.

Just as she surmised, he was at the barbecue, with Alma, whose other young man was not present. She hung on to Scott's arm, flirting with him, using her big dark eyes as only the experienced knew how, and Jane could well see how he came by his opinion of women. Depressed, and feeling so weary from loss of sleep that she could have left the barbecue and gone to her room, Jane strolled away from the chattering throng standing about under the palms, holding plates of food cooked by the natives who had made fires on the beach. Just a few minutes' break would revive her, she thought, finding a quiet corner of the garden away from the glare of lights illuminating the lawns and shrubberies. The bench was set under a dainty pink poui tree and Jane rested her head against its trunk.

Voices caught her ears and she shrank back, out of sight of the path.

'I think I must leave Coral Gables, Margaret. It isn't possible for me to stay, not under the circumstances.' The speaker was Gwen – the young receptionist who had come to the hotel the week after the arrival of Jane and Les. Les had engaged her, choosing her from among six applicants, after Mrs. Bakewell, the existing receptionist, had given in her notice, deciding she did not want to work under a new manager. Gwen – wanting to leave already? Les would be so upset, Jane felt sure, as he often praised her efficiency and remarked on the charming manner she adopted with the guests.

'You've been very foolish, Gwen.' Margaret, one of

the girls employed to run the various tours which were part of the service offered to the guests, spoke with sympathy in her voice as she added, 'It hurts like hell, loving someone out of reach. I know, because it happened to me once.'

'He was married?'

'Yes. And like you, I decided to get out, to take myself right away. It's the only thing to do. You get over it in time, whereas if you stay around it gets gradually worse.'

'I wish I'd never come! Sometimes I think I can't go – can't bear not to see him, ever. But at other times I know I must go.' A pause and then, 'They never seem in love . . .'

'They must be; they've only been married a few months. Mr. Coates had to be married in order to get the post . . .' Margaret's voice gradually faded as the two girls strolled on, hidden from Jane's eyes by the thick bougainvillaea hedge, on the other side of which they were now walking.

Jane sat very still, shocked by what she had heard. Gwen in love with Les – and believing him to be married! She had sounded so unhappy, so hopeless. Jane's own dejection spread like an enveloping cloak. What a damnable situation! Gwen was so sweet, and although Les was not interested in her at present, he could be, later, if only Gwen would stay.

'The web of lies,' Jane whispered to herself. 'How does one extricate oneself? We should never have done it. I knew all along that complications must result.'

But never in her wildest imaginings could she have foreseen all this. Should she speak to Scott and ask him to allow the whole thing to be cleared up? It only needed his consent, and his promise that Les would be convinced that he was forgiven and that there was no need for him to throw up his job— Jane cut her musings at this point. Les was too vulnerable; he would be so thoroughly ashamed that nothing would induce him to remain as manager of the hotel.

A deep sigh escaped her as she got up and made her way back to the shore. The picture of Alma hanging on to Scott's arm did nothing to help lift her spirits and it needed only old Mr. Bradshawe to seek her out to bring her to the point of tears.

'Ah, there you are, my dear Mrs. Coates. I've been looking for you the whole evening. Will you come into the bar and have a drink with me?'

She nodded wearily.

'Of course, Mr. Bradshawe.' They began to walk back to the hotel. 'Are you enjoying the barbecue?'

'Very much indeed. The food's marvellous. But I missed you. I like young company – and especially pretty young company!' He gave a laugh and she shuddered. At eighty years of age he was still upright, square of shoulder and sprightly on his legs. He had sought Jane out from the moment of entering the hotel, when, Gwen having been off colour, Jane had told her to go to bed and had taken over her job for the rest of the evening. She disliked Mr. Bradshawe on sight, but of course she did not show it. On the contrary, she was polite as ever, producing the necessary smile of welcome and expressing the hope that he would enjoy his stay with them. He was sure he would, had been his swift response, and he had patted Jane's bare arm in the most familiar way. His arm would have gone round her shoulders now, but she forestalled him, making sure that she stepped aside each time he came close to her.

They were sitting in the bar when Scott and Alma entered, and with a smile Scott asked if he could join them. In spite of the coldness that had developed between her and Scott, Jane threw him a grateful glance, to which he responded with a faint inclination of his head.

'I seem always to be rescuing you from old fogeys,' he whispered in her ear a few minutes later. 'How do you manage to get yourself tied up with all these senior citizens?'

'There's something about me that appeals to them, apparently.'

'Scott darling, what are you whispering for?' Alma complained just as he was about to bend towards Jane's ear again. 'Have you and Mrs. Coates got a secret?'

'How did you guess?' he laughed. 'Indeed we have.'

'Then I want to be let into it! I demand to be let into it!'

Scott regarded her as he might regard a fractious child whom he would dearly have loved to spank. Jane felt a little lighter from the realization of this, as it did seem that Scott cared little or nothing about this girl with whom he was going about.

'You demand, Alma?' said Scott softly, and the girl went a trifle red. 'Surely you know me better than to use a word like that?'

Alma pouted; Jane transferred her glance and saw that Scott was frowning and looking decidedly impatient. Serve him right! He should have more sense than to go about with a girl like Alma Bonsall.

'You're not in a very nice mood tonight, Scott! I think I'll ask you to take me home.'

'Home?'

'Well, to where I'm staying.' She seemed to have had too much to drink, Jane thought, and the girl's next words strengthened the idea. 'I live on the island of St. Vincent, Mrs. Coates, if that's of any interest to you.'

'It isn't,' Jane could not resist saying, and Scott's lips twitched.

'It isn't? But how rude. You should be interested in all your guests!'

'But you're not one of our guests, Miss Bonsall,' pointed out Jane sweetly.

'For tonight I am! Scott brought me, so we're both your guests!'

Jane looked at Scott; his face was a mask now and she gathered that Alma had no idea that Scott had any financial interest in Coral Gables.

'You're staying somewhere else, though, Miss Bonsall.'

'At the—' She stopped and creased her brow. 'I never can remember the name. But it's a rotten place! I've asked to come here, but your receptionist will insist that you're full, and I'm quite sure you're not!'

'I'm quite sure we are, Miss Bonsall.'

'Oh, well, it doesn't matter. I shall be going home the day after tomorrow.' She leant towards Scott; Jane had a whiff of heavy exotic perfume. 'You'll be coming too, won't you, darling?'

Scott nodded his head.

'I believe I shall be going over to St. Vincent the day

after tomorrow.'

'I'm so glad. I do hate travelling alone.' A dazzling smile went the rounds. Mr. Bradshawe glowed and asked Alma how it was that she and he had not met before now.

'Mrs. Coates knows that I very much enjoy pretty female company.'

Scott and Jane exchanged glances.

'I've only come for the barbecue,' purred Alma. 'Are you all alone here?'

'Quite alone. But Mrs. Coates is around in the evenings and keeps me company, don't you, my dear?'

'I try, Mr. Bradshawe.' A forced smile accompanied her words. 'Often, though, I have other things to do.'

Alma yawned elegantly behind a perfectly manicured hand.

'Scott darling, I'm so very tired. Would you take me back to my hotel?' She paused, and as he did not speak at once she added in a softly purring tone, 'Or I might stay at your beautiful new house . . .?'

'Is that what you want?' If he noticed the expression of disgust on Jane's face he chose to ignore it.

'I'd love it! Haven't I just said how horrid my hotel is?'

'You have, Alma, but you're very hard to please, remember.'

'I know I shall be more than pleased with your new house.'

'You've seen it already.'

'But never slept there.' The sultry voice seemed, to Jane's most critical ears, to hold some hidden meaning. She glanced at Scott and her eyes plainly told him what she thought of Alma. His mouth quivered, and Jane knew he was inwardly amused.

'Then, my dear,' said Scott with a smile for Alma, 'you shall sleep there tonight.'

Jane actually gave a start. Despite the trend of conversation she had not until this moment believed that Scott would take the girl to his home. Her wildly expanding imagination brought unbearable pain. By what strange quirk of fate had she come to fall in love with the man that Scott now was, yet she had turned from him when he was good and kind and decent morally? She must stop dwelling on the past, she told herself sternly. She had thrown away the gold and now not even the dross was within her grasp.

He was rising to his feet; he picked up a wrap that Alma had thrown across the back of her chair.

'We're going?' Alma rose and pushed an arm through his. 'Good night, Mrs. Coates – Mr. Bradshawe. We might meet again some time.'

He went coy and the colour mounted his cheeks.

'I sincerely hope so. Yes, indeed I do. Good-bye for now.'

Scott's eyes met those of Jane. His inner amusement was there still, but his voice was untinged by this humour as he said,

'Mrs. Coates, you look extremely tired. I think you should trot off to bed, don't you agree, Mr. Bradshawe?'

The old man frowned.

'Well – er—'

'I knew you would agree with me. Mrs. Coates . . .' A sweep of his hand indicated that she should precede him and gratefully she obeyed the silent invitation.

With a smile she said good night to the old man and walked away with Scott and his companion.

'Thank you,' she murmured softly while Alma was busy at a mirror, combing her hair. 'I'm grateful to you.'

'No trouble at all. Good night, Jane. I'll see you in the morning.'

She merely nodded, dejected and at the same time sick with disgust as she saw Scott and Alma going off together, to spend the night at his home.

And later, she added anger to her other emotions as she lay awake in her bed, tossing and turning, unable to sleep because of the vivid picture which her imagination put before her eyes.

## CHAPTER SIX

WHEN Jane arrived at Driftwood House the following morning she fully expected to find that Scott had not yet started work, but she was mistaken. He was in his study, but he did happen to stifle a yawn as after knocking she entered in response to his 'Come in'.

'Good morning,' she said stiffly, her notebook in her hand. She felt embarrassed, and angry because of it. He should be embarrassed, not she. On the contrary, he was looking perfectly cool and self-assured – except for being tired, that was, she thought.

'Good morning, Jane.' Scott eyed her intently, then indicated a chair opposite to where he was sitting, at his desk. She sat down, and stared at her notebook. Where was Alma? she wondered. Still in bed, probably. 'There are several letters for you to take down,' he said casually, 'and another report to type.'

For the next twenty minutes or so she was occupied, but her mind kept wandering to Alma and twice she had to ask Scott to repeat what he had said.

'What's the matter with you this morning?' he snapped, frowning at her. 'Concentrate!'

Jane bit her lip and tried her best to keep her mind on her work, but once again she failed and this time the imperious voice of her employer demanded to know what was wrong. His eyes were hard; his mouth and jaw took on lines she had never seen before. And all at once her lip trembled and she found herself blinking rapidly in order to hold back the tears which threatened to fall. She thought unhappily, 'He wasn't like this with Alma,' and then she frowned at the intrusion, because in spite of the way she felt she had no wish to be classed with a woman who would brazenly ask to sleep at a man's house.

'If you'll excuse me,' she said huskily, 'I'm not very well – I mean, I have a headache . . .'

'A headache?' Scott looked intently at her. 'Is that the reason for your tears?'

Vexedly she brushed a hand across her eyes. Absurdly she said,

'I'm not crying.'

'No? Then you must have something in your eyes.'

At this she glared at him, her dejection for the moment forgotten.

'Do you need to taunt me?' she flashed. 'What is your object? Are you getting your own back for what I did to you four years ago? If so then it's disgustingly petty!' Immediately the words were out she regretted them, since they were hardly what one would say to one's employer.

His eyes were narrowed; they flickered over her for a brief while before settling on her face. She stared fascinated at the strange unfathomable expression which she had noticed once or twice before. What were his thoughts? she wondered, Alma forgotten because the scene belonged to herself and Scott alone. It was, in some indefinable way, intimate, owing to the silence and the way Scott was looking at her, and because of her own feelings and the vital awareness that despite her anger and dejection she was acutely affected by the man by whom she was once so loved that he had asked her to marry him.

'I think, Jane,' he said at last, 'that you know me well enough to be sure I'd never indulge in reprisals. Such conduct would be disgustingly petty, as you remarked.' Soft the tone – and with an almost gentle edge to it. Jane caught her breath; it was a little sob, and her lip began to quiver tremulously again. Where was her poise? – the strength and self-assurance she had always been able to maintain in the old days? She it was who exhibited superiority – and even arrogance – in her dealings with Scott. He it was who seemed faintly lacking in self-confidence, even becoming irresolute at times. 'I think you owe me an apology,' he was saying, breaking into her unhappy musings, and she inclined her head in an involuntary gesture of agreement.

'I'm sorry,' she said in quiet husky tones. 'I don't know what made me say it.'

Scott turned from her suddenly – just as if he were unwilling to reveal his expression. His voice was still gentle when he spoke, but it was firm too, and what he said was definitely an order.

'You're going back to Coral Gables – and going to bed.' Coming round again, he regarded her intently. 'You haven't slept, have you?'

She shook her head without hesitation.

'No,' she admitted, 'I haven't.'

Again that regard as he took in the brightness of her eyes, and the quivering mouth.

'Why didn't you sleep, Jane?' he inquired softly after a pause.

'It – was the heat,' she responded, hoping that sounded feasible. He was so observant, she had several times noticed, and now she found herself fearing he might just make a guess at the real reason for her wakefulness. He shrugged his shoulders and said, without much interest,

'If you say it was the heat then it was the heat.'

She looked swiftly at him. His face was inscrutable.

'There isn't any need for me to leave,' she murmured presently, only now taking in the full import of his decision to send her home. He was anxious about her, obviously, and the knowledge acted most oddly upon her, causing a tear to fall and trickle down her cheek. Scott frowned on noticing it, and once again turned from her. She was puzzled by his whole manner. Could it be that, despite the formidable exterior she had come to know, he was still the same kind and gentle person underneath? Automatically she shook her head. No; the change was complete, Jane felt certain of this. His anxiety merely stemmed from the thought that, should he not send her home now, she might be ill and unable to come in to work for several days. This she knew would inconvenience him, and the inconvenience was his sole concern.

'I'll take you back in the car,' he said, ignoring her words. 'Go and collect your things.'

'But—' The protest was cut by his expression even before he spoke.

'Go and get your things, Jane,' he repeated, very quietly. 'I'll be outside waiting for you.'

The drive to Coral Gables was a silent one, with Scott preoccupied and Jane's thoughts once more reverting to Alma. Dejection crept in on Jane and this, in addition to the tiredness possessing her, resulted in an involuntary sigh escaping her. Scott turned his head but remained silent. She glanced at his stern set profile and remembered the kindly face she had once known. She saw again the softness of the mouth, the tender light that seemed ever to be in his eyes when he looked at her; she recalled vividly the smile which came so spontaneously to his lips whenever he and Jane met. To him at that time she was his girl, the one he dearly loved – the one with whom he was more than willing to share his life.

Jane swallowed something tight that had settled in her throat. How could she have been such a fool?

'Here we are.' The sentence was abrupt, spoken merely to break the deep silence that had endured throughout the short journey from Driftwood house to Coral Gables. 'Remember what I said – go to bed.'

'Thank you for letting me come home,' she said huskily. 'I'll be quite all right in the morning.'

He glanced indifferently at her as, leaning across her, he opened the car door. She got out and he closed it. She would have spoken, to express her thanks once more, but Scott had already let in the clutch and the car was moving away.

Les happened to come along at that moment and his expression immediately changed, concern entering his eyes as he looked searchingly at his sister.

'Something wrong?' he inquired anxiously just as she was about to explain.

'I felt tired, and Scott let me come home.'

Les's eyes widened.

'You felt tired? He knew this?'

'He guessed that I hadn't slept.' She answered dully, wishing she had been able to escape these questions.

'He must have been very observant,' commented

Les, watching her closely.

Jane nodded her head.

'I wasn't concentrating on my work,' she admitted. 'He was bound to notice that something was wrong.'

'He brought you home himself?'

'That's right. I expect he thought it would be quicker than telephoning for a taxi.'

Les was still watching her intently, his expression thoughtful, and a little troubled.

'I wonder why he should be so concerned about you?' he murmured, almost to himself. 'I'm sure no other boss would have troubled to drive you home himself.'

'It wasn't far.'

'I know, but there must be some reason for his anxiety about you ...' Les tailed off thoughtfully, a frown appearing on his brow. 'If he should still care—' He broke the sentence sharply, and looked at her. In spite of her efforts at calm Jane felt the colour rise in her cheeks. 'I seem to remember,' continued Les when she did not speak, 'that you evaded a direct answer when I asked how you now felt about Scott?'

Carelessly she shrugged, hoping the gesture was producing the desired effect.

'There could never be anything between Scott and me now. I told you that, Les.'

He remained doubtful, lapsing into a mood of speculation.

'I still think it odd that he's never married,' he commented at length.

'He's having a good time instead.' The words were difficult to voice and she avoided her brother's eyes as she spoke. 'He admitted to me that he prefers this sort of life to marriage.'

Les was shaking his head.

'He doesn't strike me as that type at all.'

She opened her mouth to tell him that Alma had slept at Driftwood House last night, but something deterred her. She had no wish that Les should learn of that particular incident. But she did say, unaware of the deep regret in her voice,

'He is that type, Les. I've told you, he's admitted it.'

'Strange that he should be so ready to do so, don't you think?'

It was Jane's turn to frown. She was more than tired now; she was drooping under the weight of a heavy languor which was only partly accounted for by her loss of sleep. Dejection was responsible for the greater part of it, and although a rest would bring relief, there was the inevitable awakening to follow.

'I don't quite know where this conversation is leading, Les – or what you're getting at. But if you don't mind, I want to go to bed. Scott brought me home so that I'd rest.'

'Evasion again?' Les shrugged then and spread his hands. 'I'll mind my own business in future,' he promised, and Jane bit her lip, aware that she had snubbed him and yet unable to find any way of eradicating the slight hurt she had caused him.

'Will you see that I'm called about tea time?' she asked.

'You don't want any lunch?'

'No, thank you, Les. I'm going to try and have a long sleep.'

To her surprise she managed to sleep until she was

called, but she lay for a while, her thoughts drifting to Scott, and for a few moments she dwelt on the position regarding her relationship with him. As things were, she was forced to be in contact with him for several hours each day, and she had to own to herself that, before very long, she must reach the point where being with him would become sheer agony. She felt trapped, and remembered that she had experienced this same feeling when first she learned that she had to work for Scott as his secretary. It were better that she leave the island now, and yet this was quite impossible. Scott had forbidden her to mention to Les that Scott knew of the deceit, and she had obeyed the command – firstly because of the way it was given, Scott's voice and expression telling her quite plainly that she would regret it if she dared to go against his wishes. But of course there was also the strong deterrent of her brother's reaction which would most likely result in his leaving the island, and the kind of job he had so long coveted.

With a deep sigh she arose at last, took a bath and dressed in a fresh crisp cotton dress, low-cut and sleeveless. She felt better, and looked better, she noticed with some satisfaction, taking a last look in the mirror before proceeding downstairs to the lounge in which tea was usually served.

It was Gwen's afternoon off and she was sitting alone on the verandah. Jane went out and joined her, escaping for once from the old people who were gathered in the lounge, waiting for their afternoon tea to be brought in.

Gwen glanced up and a smile fluttered; plainly she was not happy, the smile obviously being forced. Jane's heart went out to her and she would have done anything to be able to inform the girl that she was Les's sister, and not his wife. But of course that was impossible and a rather awkward silence fell between the two girls, broken at last by Jane who, just for something to say, asked Gwen what she had been doing with her time off.

'I went for a stroll on the beach,' she replied, without much interest.

'I don't see you swimming at all?'

'I do swim – but not here. It's no fun swimming alone.' The dejection was all too apparent and Jane frowned and bit her lip.

'We'll go together next time you're off. That will be on Friday, I believe?'

Gwen nodded. Her eyes, brooding and shadowed, were fixed on the shimmering expanse of crystal clear water stretching away to the horizon where it met the sky, cobalt blue and flecked with fine-weather cumulus clouds.

'Will you really come swimming with me?' she asked unexpectedly, turning her head to look at Jane.

'Of course. I too shall be glad of the company.'

A small pause and then, hesitantly,

'Your husband – Mr. Coates – doesn't swim with you?'

'He doesn't have much time, as you have probably discovered by now.'

'Yes . . .' Another pause. 'You haven't been married very long, have you?'

A sigh escaped Jane. This situation was damnable.

'No, Gwen, we haven't been married long.' Looking up, Jane saw with relief that the waiter was approaching with Gwen's tea tray. 'Do you mind if I join you?' she asked.

The girl hesitated briefly, then shook her head.

'Not at all, Mrs. Coates.'

'You want the same, madam?' from the waiter, glancing at Jane.

'Yes, please, Dick. But not quite so much butter on the bread.'

'Very good, madam.'

It was not a very pleasant meal, for Gwen was silent and even morose, speaking only when it was absolutely necessary. Jane persevered but naturally it was a strain, endeavouring to pursue a conversation with someone intent on maintaining a brooding silence.

'Mrs. Coates,' said Gwen with sudden decision just as the last cup of tea was being drunk, 'I want to give in my notice.'

Silence fell. Jane sat watching the girl's expression, particularly noting the slight movement of her lips and the rapidity with which she blinked, revealing just how close to tears she was. There must be some way of handling this situation, thought Jane, feeling – quite without any valid reason – that eventually Les was bound to notice this pretty girl with the sincere blue eyes and soft compassionate mouth.

'What reason have you for wanting to leave?' Jane inquired at length, realizing all at once that this question would naturally be expected of her.

'I – I—' Gwen broke off and turned her head to one side, unwilling to let her companion see how deeply affected she was. 'I just want to leave, Mrs. Coates,' she managed presently. 'Please don't ask for any further explanation.'

'Mr. Coates will require one,' she reminded the girl gently.

'I can't give him one!' Emphatic tones and sharp. Gwen kept her head turned away from Jane as she added, 'The reason is private, and one I couldn't possibly disclose.'

'I see. When are you wanting to go?'

'I expect I shall have to give a month's notice.'

'I expect you will,' agreed Jane. 'Where are you thinking of going?'

'Home.'

'To England? But you've been here in Barbados for some time – so my husband tells me.'

'That's right. I've worked in another hotel for four years. I left only because it changed hands and I didn't like my new boss.'

'Ah, yes, I remember.' A pause. 'Must you go home?' she then asked, and Gwen nodded vigorously.

'Yes, I must.' A movement caught her attention and she glanced up. Les smiled at the girls in turn and then sat down.

'I see you've almost finished,' he observed. 'Don't rush off, though,' he begged, 'I hate eating alone.' He beckoned to the native waiter who came silently and with a flashing smile. 'Tea and cakes – and just one sandwich,' he said.

An awkward silence descended and, puzzled, Les glanced interrogatingly at his sister. She in turn looked at Gwen, whose glance clearly said, 'You tell him, please.'

'Gwen wants to leave us, Les,' Jane informed him, and a frown came swiftly to his brow.

'Whatever for?' he inquired of Gwen. 'You have a complaint?'

'No, Mr. Coates,' she whispered, averting her head. 'It's just that I've made up my mind to leave Barbados.'

Watching him closely, Jane saw her brother swallow hard, heard him say in tones that were a mingling of persuasion and regret,

'Is this a firm decision, Gwen? Won't you reconsider?'

She shook her head.

'No – I can't stay, Mr. Coates.'

After a long moment of silence he shrugged his shoulders and said resignedly,

'Very well, Gwen. But we're very sorry to be losing you so soon.' He looked at her. 'It's all very sudden. You were most keen to get the post.'

'Yes, I was, at that time.'

'Something must have happened?' Despite his air of resignation Les was persisting, thought Jane, and wondered if it were possible that already he had begun to see Gwen in another light besides that of his employee.

'As I've said, I'm leaving Barbados.' Gwen glanced away, avoiding his eyes. 'I won't change my mind, Mr. Coates.'

'No, I see that you won't.' He gave a small sigh. 'Your notice will have to start from the end of next week, Gwen. You understand that?'

'I thought I need give only one month's notice?'

'From the end of this month,' he told her firmly.

'So I have to stay for another six weeks?'

'Almost.' His eyes searched her face when at length

she turned to meet his gaze. 'I hope you won't let me down?'

'No – oh, no, Mr. Coates,' she returned quickly. 'I'd never do that.'

'Thank you,' was all he said, giving his attention to the food the waiter had just put before him. Jane poured his tea, while Gwen rose, excused herself, and left them. 'Why should she want to go?' Les glanced at Jane. 'Did she give you any clue as to the reason for this sudden decision?'

After a moment's hesitation Jane said,

'No, Les, she didn't.' But something in the way she spoke caused his eyes to narrow.

'Are you sure?'

'Quite sure.'

'I'm not satisfied,' he almost snapped.

'Gwen never gave me the slightest clue as to why she's leaving,' returned Jane, looking directly at him.

Les paused thoughtfully.

'It's said that it takes one woman to understand another,' he said at length. 'Do you yourself have any ideas about her decision?' He watched her closely and she felt the colour rise in her cheeks as the lie forced itself to her lips.

'No – why should I?'

'I don't know why you should, but I'm not at all convinced that you haven't any ideas. There's something I don't understand.' He was vexed and for a fleeting moment Jane debated on whether or not to repeat what she had overheard. But she decided to keep her knowledge to herself, as she realized she could embarrass Les by disclosing it. After all, she had not been given any indication that he might be attracted to the girl. 'Well,' he was saying shortly, 'aren't you going to comment?'

At a loss, Jane shook her head, and it was with a deep sigh of relief that she saw one of the hotel porters coming towards her brother, a message obviously on his lips.

'Mr. Coates, you're wanted on the telephone.'

'Thank you.' With a glance at his sister Les rose; the next moment she was alone, thinking about the situation and feeling more dejected than ever, because it did seem that Les was more than ordinarily upset by Gwen's decision to leave.

So greatly did the matter affect her that, impelled to tell someone about it, she mentioned it to Scott the following morning immediately she arrived at Driftwood House.

'I know I shouldn't trouble you with it,' she ended when with a lifting of his brows he indicated a question as to why she had come to him. 'But in fact you're the only one I could speak to – and I just had to speak to someone.'

'And what,' he inquired suavely, 'do you expect me to do about it?'

Vaguely she shook her head.

'Nothing, really . . .' She lifted her beautiful eyes to his. 'You wouldn't consent to—?' Again she shook her head, frowning heavily.

'A full disclosure of the truth? No, my dear Jane, I wouldn't.' So implacable the tone and firm the jaw. 'At present it doesn't serve my purpose to have the truth disclosed.'

'Serve your purpose?' she echoed, recalling her previous impression that she had been led into a trap. 'As things are,' she continued slowly and perceptively, 'you have a hold over me.' It was a statement and for a moment he made no comment. But at last he said,

'I do possess a certain power over you.' His blue eyes regarded her intently, and glimmered with satisfaction on noting her fluctuating colour. 'I haven't altogether abandoned the idea of you and me finding pleasure together. And should I decide that we shall be lovers then this power I have over you will render your own protestations somewhat weak . . . should you make any protestations, that is,' he added with a strange inflection in his voice.

Her pulse fluttered alongside a tug of anger. Had he guessed how she felt about him? – and become confident of her surrender because of that guess?

'I should most certainly protest!' she flashed. 'And even the hold you have over me wouldn't influence me to throw away my ideals!'

'Ideals?' he sneered. 'They're as old-fashioned as marriage.'

Jane's lip quivered in spite of herself. If only he knew how such cynicism hurt – piercing as the cruellest thorn. But he wouldn't care, she decided unhappily. The time when he cared for her feelings was long since past – as far from reach as the man she had then known.

'Is isn't clever to be so cynical, Scott,' she told him at last. 'There are still many good people in the world.'

'By people I assume you're really referring to women?'

'You appear to regard all women as – as easy.' It took a little effort to voice the final word, but she managed it, even holding his gaze as she did so.

'All women are easy.'

'Perhaps I should go and get on with my work,' she returned dully. 'This conversation's taking a very different direction from what I intended.'

The blue eyes smiled faintly.

'You wanted to talk about this Gwen and your brother?'

'I wish I could find some way of helping them.'

'Them? You appear to have received no indication that your brother is in any way interested in the girl.'

'He seemed rather distressed at the idea of her leaving.'

'I expect that's because she's a good employee. One likes to keep that kind if one possibly can.'

'I'm sure it was more than that.'

'I doubt it. In any case, there's nothing to stop your brother having an affair with the girl. Haven't I already said that marriage is old-fashioned?'

'Les wouldn't dream of having an affair!' retorted Jane indignantly, ignoring his question about marriage. 'Besides, you forget, he's supposed to be married. Gwen's leaving because she believes him to be married.'

To her surprise a laugh escaped Scott and the blue eyes lighted with humour in that most attractive way which brought back with deep nostalgia so many memories which Jane had believed to be dead. It was strange, she thought, that she had ever been able to resist this and other numerous attractions which the old Scott possessed. But she had been so concerned by having a husband with more than ordinary strength of character that his other, more important qualities had registered only vaguely at the time. Yet now they drifted back to her and she realized that in some deep recess of her unconscious they had found themselves a permanent place. This, she believed on pondering it, had been the reason why no other man had ever appealed to her during the whole of those four years. She looked up into his mocking eyes . . . and wished with all her heart she could tell him what was in her mind.

'I can't agree that your brother would not have an affair,' Scott was saying with a hint of satire. 'Any man would have an affair if the chance came his way.'

'And Gwen?' she countered angrily. 'You believe she would agree to an affair – with a married man whose wife she knew?'

Again Scott laughed.

'You and your brother *have* got yourselves into a mess, haven't you?'

Jane flushed guiltily.

'You perhaps won't believe it, but I hated the deceit.'

'You did?' drily and with a trace of scepticism.

'I'm here only because Les would have been so disappointed at losing the post. He had a girl and we believed she was serious about marrying him. That was why he applied for the post in the first place—' She stopped and glanced apologetically at him. 'I've told you this before, haven't I?'

He nodded.

'Soon after I'd disclosed the fact of my knowledge about your being the sister and not the wife of the manager of Coral Gables.' He paused a moment and a frown settled on his forehead. 'So had he been able to bring this girl with him as his wife you'd never have come?'

'Of course I wouldn't.'

He looked intently at her.

'Are you sorry you came?' he asked, a strange note in his voice.

She averted her head, unwilling for him to see her expression. For she knew not whether she was sorry. True, much heartache would have been avoided, but somehow she could not truthfully say that she regretted having met Scott again – this in spite of the enormous changes that had taken place in his personality. He was speaking, softly yet insistently, and when she still refused either to answer or to raise her head she felt his finger under her chin.

'So you're not sorry,' he murmured, and in the triumph of the moment he took her in his arms and kissed her. 'We *shall* become lovers,' he told her exultantly, crushing her protesting body to him again. 'You won't be able to help yourself—'

'I shall!' she cried, endeavouring to pull away from him but failing. 'I'll never consent to anything so wrong!'

'Wrong?' he laughed. 'How can it be wrong when it's natural?' Jane could not speak for the pain and disgust within her, and Scott continued, 'You will consent, eventually.'

'Then wait and see!'

'I'm thinking I'll not wait long,' he murmured, forcing his lips to hers. The kiss was long and ardent, and persuasive in a way that spelled experience. 'You're too desirable. I even believe I prefer you to Alma, and that's flattery indeed. Why, my dear Jane, how delectably you blush. Is anger the reason, or have I embarrassed you? Or it could be my flattery—'

'I hate you,' she whispered fiercely. 'I think you're the most detestable man I've ever met!'

'You do?' Imperturbably he held her from him, his cool blue eyes questioning, yet mocking too, and bright with humour. 'You really hate me? Now, tell me why you so suddenly hate me?'

'Because of the change, if you must know!'

'Ah . . .' Strangely, he appeared to be inordinately satisfied by her answer. 'So you don't like the change?' She could only shake her head dumbly, aware that her eyes were far too bright because of the tears behind them caused by the deep distress within her. 'I had hoped the change would be for the better,' he was saying, and she was more than a little suspicious that he was suppressing laughter. 'If you remember, my dear Jane, you had no patience with an inexperienced man – oh, you didn't say this outright. You were in fact nicely subtle in the way you worded your complaints as to my character. Nevertheless, it was quite obvious that you despised the type of man I was, and it would seem that your ideal not only had to be a tyrant who would reduce you to vassalage but also a man who had been around – a rake, in fact.' Humour faded as he spoke until, at the end, his eyes were glinting with anger. Jane shook her head bewilderedly, astonished that he should be speaking like this to her. What did it matter what she had said in the past? It should by rights have been forgotten long ago by Scott who, she recalled, had actually thanked her for turning him down. He was grateful to have escaped the marriage net, he implied, having gone on to say that a man could enjoy all the advantages without taking upon himself the burden which was the normal lot of the married man.

He still held her close; she made a sharp twist with the intention of drawing from his embrace, but his arms instantly tightened, masterfully and causing her real physical pain. She winced, but his hold remained firm.

'Let me go,' she cried. 'I came here to work, not to – to—' She stopped, vague about what she had meant to say.

'—make love,' finished Scott on a quizzical note. 'It is a little early in the morning, I admit, but you're so very tempting, especially in this mood of non-compliance. Mind you,' he went on still allowing her to feel his strength as she made another attempt to free herself, 'I rather enjoy a struggle. I believe women do too, since they often act as you're acting now. Is your resistance genuine – or designed to lead me on?' He was laughing at her, enjoying her helplessness as she attempted to escape from his hold. He bent his head and kissed her. 'It's rather enjoyable to have a hold over you, Jane,' he said when she made no answer to his question. 'You can be sure that I'll use to the full the power it affords me.'

## CHAPTER SEVEN

DURING the next few days Jane had a dread of any further demonstrations by Scott, whose threat, at the time, had seemed not to be lightly made. However, the days passed uneventfully until Thursday afternoon when Scott told Jane she could have the following day off as he was going to St. Vincent.

He brought Alma back with him on his return and they dined at the hotel on the Monday evening. As Alma's other man friend was not present Scott danced with her the whole time – until half past ten, that was, when Jane saw them strolling away to one of the darkest and loneliest parts of the grounds.

On the Tuesday Jane asked if she could leave half an hour early as she was seeing a man who had a car for sale. He was bringing it to Coral Gables and Jane hoped it would suit her requirements.

'I said I'd vet a car for you,' Scott reminded her. 'Had you forgotten?'

'No—' She hesitated. 'I thought perhaps you'd changed your mind after – after the way you were the other day.'

A laugh lit his eyes.

'That?' he said carelessly. 'It was merely a diversion. You looked particularly attractive and I was tempted to hold you in my arms and kiss you. It has nothing to do with more practical and important things like buying a car. Of course I shall look it over for you. It's being brought to Coral Gables this afternoon, you say?'

'Yes; the man can't bring it any other time,' she added apologetically.

'That's all right. We can be there.' He glanced at his wrist watch as he spoke.

'You're giving me a lift home?'

'If I'm going to Coral Gables then obviously I shall give you a lift.'

Sitting beside him in the car a short while later, Jane dwelt on what he had said about that memorable scene's merely being a diversion. That he was playing with her was more than ever apparent, and so piqued did she become that she found herself searching for some means of retaliating. The method by which she could achieve this retaliation was vague in the extreme, but was to take more concrete form when, the following week, she met the young and handsome Hal Charlton at the Yacht Club, the island's most important social club.

The occasion of the meeting was a Yacht Club dance and Jane had been invited through David who, with Susan, had attended many such dances. Looking her superb best in a long white dress with sequin trimmings that glittered in the soft muted light, Jane was introduced to Hal very soon after her arrival.

'I told you you'd meet some presentable young men at the Yacht Club,' teased Susan, and went on to add that Jane must make sure she didn't fall – as she was married!

Well, she wouldn't fall, thought Jane, but Hal was certainly attractive and it was flattering to know that he was interested in her. He seemed unable to take his eyes off her when David made the introductions, and his murmured 'How do you do,' seemed a purely automatic response.

He was soon asking her to dance, and as his steps and Jane's were in complete harmony Jane thoroughly enjoyed every dance. She tried not to think about Scott and Alma, who were also present, dancing together for most of the time, but inevitably she found them in her line of vision at times and then a wave of dejection would flood over her.

'I must take you out to dine,' Hal was saying when together he and Jane sat eating their refreshments. 'I'm so glad I met you.' His enthusiasm and spontaneity were refreshing after the cynicism and mockery invariably displayed by Scott whenever he was with her. Jane found herself agreeing to go out with Hal and the date was made long before the evening came to an end.

Scott came over and invited her to dance; she slid into his arms and he whirled her away into the centre of the hall. He seemed in a temper, she thought, frowning inwardly. Had Alma been playing him up? Serve him right if she had! She was even now laughing up at her partner with that coquettish glance and smile which she so often used with Scott.

'Are you enjoying yourself?' inquired Scott at length.

'Very much.' And she added a trifle acidly, 'I expect you are too?'

Strangely, he made no answer, appearing to be preoccupied and still not in the most pleasant of moods. Something had gone wrong, obviously, something that had caused him considerable annoyance.

'Thank you,' he said brusquely as the music stopped and he turned to leave her. Hal was at her side instantly, and Jane could not be quite sure whether or not Scott had fleetingly turned his head as the young man spoke.

'I'm claiming you for all the rest, Jane.'

And he did. But later he asked Jane if she would like some fresh air, and on her ready agreement they strolled out into the gardens and beyond, through the very spacious grounds of the club. The dark calm sea of Carlisle Bay lapped gently at the pale sands, and above the sky was alive with stars. It was a typical Caribbean evening, with the air warm and heady and the music of a steel band drifting out from the club.

On their return they strolled past the tennis courts and crossed smooth wide lawns, stopping by the beautiful hedge of Pride of Barbados while Jane touched some of the bright orange-coloured flowers. Hal was looking at her appreciatively, she knew; he was not averse to a flirtation – she knew this too. During the evening he had put questions to her about her husband and she had been forced to tell several deliberate lies, and even more white ones. Didn't she mind having to come to a function like this without her husband? he had asked almost at the beginning, when they were having their very first dance together.

'No, I don't mind. He has to be on duty, so there's nothing we can do about it.'

Hal had looked strangely at her.

'You don't feel you should stay with him?' By the way he spoke Jane guessed that, somehow, he had been informed that she and Les had not been 'married' very long.

'We both need recreation. Les goes out when I'm on duty.' Which wasn't quite true since Jane no longer worked at the hotel, not since becoming Scott's secretary.

'I see. Oh, well, let's forget your husband and enjoy the evening.'

And now, standing by the hedge, he moved a little closer and slipped an arm around her shoulders. She was just about to twist away when she spotted Scott and Alma, coming towards the place where they stood; instead of repulsing Hal she turned her face up invitingly and, as she expected, he kissed her.

Scott and Alma passed within a few feet of them and it was impossible that they could have missed the little scene of intimacy.

That, decided Jane, would put Scott in his true place – that of her employer and nothing more, it being most unlikely that he would ever speak again of forcing her into an affair with him. He would brand her as flighty, perhaps, but on the other hand he might decide that she was genuinely attracted to Hal. Jane sincerely hoped it would be this latter.

However, she was not prepared for what he had to say to her the following morning when she arrived at Driftwood House in the little car which Scott had not hesitated in advising her to buy. She saw him standing on the verandah as she parked at the end of the long avenue of cabbage palms. He had been gazing abstractedly across the croquet lawn to a dazzling border where hibiscus and oleander and poinsettia bloomed beneath the slender casuarina trees and the sweetly-perfumed frangipanis.

But his head turned, slowly, as he watched the car being brought to a standstill. Jane offered a smile and a bright 'good morning', but received nothing more friendly than an abrupt nod in return.

For a breathless moment she stood at the foot of the verandah steps looking up at him, standing by one of the fluted coral pillars around which grew a beautiful bougainvillaea vine. She was deeply affected by his magnetism; and even his forbidding exterior was a vital stimulus which accentuated her yearning for him.

'I want to speak to you,' he said in a very soft tone which set her nerves tingling. Slowly she mounted the steps.

'You – d-do?' Instinctively she knew he was about to mention last night, and the kissing incident, and her colour fluctuated in consequence. The steely blue eyes narrowed, perceptively and with piercing intensity. How very overpowering he was – standing there, like a judge! Inevitably a back-switch of memory produced a picture of Scott at twenty-six, a man in every sense, it was true; but with Jane he had been a little unsure of himself, a trifle anxious in case she should turn down his offer of marriage. In consequence he had carefully refrained from exhibiting any sign of his innate strength of character which Jane now knew to her cost included all the mastery she could ever desire – and much more besides!

'Last night,' he continued in the same dangerously quiet accents. 'What sort of an exhibition was that? – allowing a complete stranger to make love to you?'

'He was not making love to me!' she cried, but her protestation was ignored.

'It would have been disgusting enough had people known you were single, but you're supposed to be married.' Accusation lay both in his voice and in the dark cold glance he directed at her. 'I do not allow any sort of scandal to attach to my employees,' he continued. 'If ever you act in so abandoned a way again I shall not hesitate to dispense both with your services and those of your brother.'

She caught her breath, dismay plucking at her senses. Nevertheless, she was not yet so subdued and afraid that she was unable to flash a retort.

'I did not act in an abandoned manner. No one even saw us—'

'*I* saw you,' he cut in frigidly, 'and so did Alma. If you're not careful you'll soon be having your name bandied around among all the young hopefuls on Barbados!'

'Oh . . .!' Fury brought two brighter spots of colour to flare above the rest. 'What a thing to say!'

'This is an island,' he reminded her tersely, his eyes flickering over her with a contemptuous expression that stabbed even as it served to swell her anger. 'Gossip travels fast.'

'No one,' she told him quiveringly, 'is going to gossip about me!'

'I imagine the gossip has already begun.'

'I don't believe you!'

'I've lived on islands longer than you,' he reminded her icily, 'and I know what happens when a woman – especially a married one – indulges in flirtations with men like Hal Charlton.'

'He has a reputation?' she queried, for the moment diverted from the main issue.

'He has,' briefly and with emphasis.

Jane looked down at her feet, feeling more unhappy than ashamed, the fact of Hal's reputation affording her a slight measure of satisfaction since she could now use him without there being any danger of his suffering hurt. And use him as she fully intended doing. Scott Kingsley was going to be kept in his place as her employer. With another man in the picture he would hardly pursue the matter of having an affair with her. Not that she really believed he meant to do so; by now she was growing a little more wise to his tactics and realizing that while they were in part a game conducted for his amusement, they also constituted a carefully-devised plan by which he was getting his own back for the damage she had done to his pride in the past.

She said after a contemplative silence,

'While I'm fully aware that you can dismiss me, I do not believe you would dismiss my brother as well. Such an action would be grossly unfair, since he's done nothing to deserve dismissal, and—' Jane broke off, casting him a sideways glance. 'I'm quite sure you'd never act in so unjust a way.'

A faint, humourless smile touched his mouth.

'Then you don't know me very well.'

She examined his expression, convinced that she had him at a disadvantage. She could press home with a reminder that he had on more than one occasion praised Les; she could remind him too of his declaration that Les would be an asset to the firm. But some inner warning impelled her to pause a moment and consider his probable reaction. She decided that silence was the best policy since the last thing she desired was to anger him. And so she merely said, and this in a rather subdued tone,

'You once mentioned that it was a wise course to keep a good employee.'

The blue eyes glinted.

'Just what are you trying to do, Jane?' inquired Scott in a very soft tone.

She feigned bewilderment.

'I don't know what you mean?'

Scott traded his smile for a disparaging twist of his lips.

'You're not obtuse,' he said, and added, 'No counter-stroke you can think up will avail you anything. Either you act in a more seemly fashion or you take the consequences.' He was the employer, stern, implacable. He was not hesitating to ensure that she was fully conscious of his power over her.

'My private life has nothing to do with my position as your employee,' she ventured, loath to capitulate after having decided that the only way to combat Scott in the particular game he played was to let him believe she had found herself a young man. 'I – er – like Hal very much,' she thought to add, just for good measure.

'Like?' he repeated harshly. 'Are you telling me you're attracted to a rake like that?'

She said, her words another daring venture,

'You seem to forget, Scott, that you yourself could be branded a rake.'

His lips snapped together; she heard him grind his teeth.

'Be very careful,' he warned darkly, his fury simmering beneath the surface. 'I'm still your employer.'

Jane hung her head. It was no use trying to argue with someone who could beat her at every turn. It was incredible that at one time she had experimentally adopted a haughty manner with him, practically ordering him to take her to one hotel to dine when he himself had chosen another. And it was more incredible still that he had pandered to her desire without argument.

'You're insisting that I don't ever see Hal again?'

'You're bound to see him again; he attends all the Yacht Club functions and you'll obviously attend many of them too. I'm merely telling you to act in a more seemly manner – and to remember you're married,' he added forcibly.

'Remember I'm married ...' She looked oddly at him. 'What you're really trying to do is restrict me – as to finding myself a young man?'

'You yourself are the one who elected to adopt the role of married woman,' he reminded her harshly. 'And it's my wish that you remember it!' His anger was clearly written in his expression; Jane knew instinctively that to carry this argument further would result merely in her own embarrassment, for undoubtedly Scott was determined to have the last word.

And so no more was said at this time, but later, when she was ready to go home, he said warningly,

'Keep in mind what I've told you. If I hear that you've been seen about with Charlton there'll be trouble.'

For a fleeting moment her eyes glinted as a retort leapt to her lips, but she bit it back and, without a word, ran down the verandah steps to her car.

On the following Sunday she went over to Bathsheba to see Susan and David. The first thing Susan mentioned was the Yacht Club dance.

'You were certainly enjoying yourself. Hal Charlton told David that he wanted to see more of you.' Susan grinned and twisted the ends of her hair in that little habit of hers. 'We're pretty sure he'll be chasing you even though he's under the impression that you're married.'

Jane coloured; she was not too sure she now wanted to cultivate the attention of Hal.

'I believe he has a reputation?'

Susan nodded, but went on to say,

'What man hasn't these days?'

'Or woman either,' supplemented her husband.

'Hal isn't any worse than any other man.' Susan looked curiously at her friend. 'Do you like him?'

'He's all right,' guardedly and in a tone that suggested the subject be dropped. But Susan obviously missed this and went on,

'Lots of girls would be flattered by the attention Hal gave you the other night.' A small pause followed. 'You know, Jane, we've been thinking that the time will come when both you and Les will decide to be frank and admit to the deception.'

Jane's eyes flickered as she met her friend's gaze.

'You and David,' she began. 'Aren't you worried about your part in the deception?'

'We have been, but we now believe that Mr. Kingsley will forgive us. You see, we've made so many improvements here that every time he comes he has nothing but praise for what we've done. It seems that before he took over the company it was being sadly neglected. He appointed Mr. Spender, who happens to be an excellent man at picking out those who really have a flair for the hotel business, hence our appointments, and yours.'

'Mr. Kingsley comes here often?'

'Quite often. He's talking of an extension, and of having private family chalets built over on that spare land. They'll be lovely, with all the trees round them and the shore only seconds away.'

'Yes, indeed. You'll then have a great deal more work, and responsibility?'

David nodded, but appeared very happy at the idea.

'We'll be managing one of the largest hotels on the island,' he said with a distinct hint of pride in his voice. 'Of course, we'll be having a much larger staff.'

'Mr. Kingsley must think a lot about you,' murmured Jane, reflecting on what Susan had just said about Scott's probable forgiveness of their part in the deception which, as Jane had prophesied at the very first, was causing so much trouble – to herself mainly, but she now suspected it was troubling Les a great deal also, for she had watched him closely with Gwen and had more than once surprised a swift frown whenever the girl's departure was mentioned.

'He's a most appreciative man, and so very kind.'

Swift astonishment appeared in Jane's expression.

'Kind?' she echoed.

'Of course he's kind. You must have noticed it, working as you do, so close to him. David was saying only the other day that you must have landed yourself one of the most attractive jobs on the island. Why, you've said yourself that he's always giving you days off. And he took you home once when you told him you'd had a sleepless night.'

'The days off he gives me are so that he can go to St.

Vincent, where he used to live,' Jane informed her in a tone gone suddenly flat. For it was patently clear that Scott's arrogance and formidable manner were kept for her alone.

'He still has his house there, but he's selling it. He goes over because his girl-friend lives there.' Susan absently twisted her hair. 'You've met Miss Bonsall, surely?'

'Yes, I've met her.' Jane hesitated. 'You have too, apparently?'

'That's right. He brings her here to dine sometimes.'

'You like her?' Jane avoided Susan's eyes as she put the question, sure that her expression would give away her own feelings for Scott.

'We think she's lovely to look at,' laughed David. 'But we're not at all sure she's right for Mr. Kingsley. We think he needs someone softer – seeing that he's that way himself.'

'That way?' disbelievingly Jane shook her head. 'I'd never call Mr. Kingsley soft.'

'Not soft exactly,' corrected Susan, looking at her husband. 'He's compassionate and sort of – gentle.'

Jane's eyes wandered pensively to the beautiful curve of the Bathsheba coastline with the rolling Atlantic breakers sweeping towards the shore and the green hills rising behind it, clothed with breadfruit trees and coconut palms and the inevitable sugar canes. Small native houses dotted the landscape, all bedecked with tropical flowers.

Compassionate and gentle . . . The words spoken by Susan repeated themselves over and over in her mind as the vision of Scott as she knew him intruded to give the lie to anything even remotely connected with compassion and gentleness. The side he showed to Jane was hard and ruthless, his manner always the employer – and most certainly not a kindly employer! On the contrary he was magisterial and demanding, fault-finding with her work and even critical of her behaviour even when she wasn't at work. True, there had been the occasion when on being told she had not slept he had appeared to be anxious, and had taken her back to Coral Gables so that she could catch up with her rest, but Jane had very soon concluded that his anxiety stemmed from the inconvenience her absence from work would cause him. Far better to let her have a few hours off work than have her off for two or three days.

'You surprise me when you say he's gentle.' Jane spoke at last, aware that some comment was expected from her. 'I – I hadn't noticed. He seems very business-like and efficient.'

'Of course he is; he must be.' Susan looked at her with an odd expression. 'Don't you like Mr. Kingsley?' she asked after a slight hesitation.

Susan had asked the question before, and in the same curious tone; Jane replied as before, in the same careless tone.

'I'm indifferent to him.'

A long silence followed, Susan and David exchanging glances more than once. When at last David spoke it was to change the subject as he reverted to Alma and whether or not she was right for Scott.

'Undoubtedly she'd be an asset socially,' he went on to concede, 'but somehow they don't seem ideally suited.'

'He must think so, though,' from Susan, reasonably, 'for otherwise he wouldn't be going out with her.'

Jane wondered what they would say were she to mention that Alma had another man-friend, one to whom Scott had not the slightest objection.

'I don't think Mr. Kingsley is interested in marrying her,' she submitted. 'He doesn't strike me as the marrying sort.'

'Most men marry eventually,' put in David with a grimace expressly for his wife. 'Mr. Kingsley'll go the way of the rest of us.'

'It was you who did the chasing,' she retorted. 'I'd told you, several times, that I was determined to remain a spinster – and keep my independence!'

'But you're glad you didn't.'

'What an opinion you have of yourself! How do you know I'm glad I didn't?'

'Because, my love, of your contented expression. There's really no other state as satisfying as that of marriage . . . if you've been lucky enough to find the right one.' He glanced at Jane. 'Don't you agree with me?'

She spread her hands.

'I'm sure you're right,' she said. 'But for myself, I can't agree or disagree, as I'm not married – nor likely to be.'

'You'll marry some day,' interposed Susan emphatically. 'I'll bet something comes of this Hal business. If you fall for one another then you'll just have to open up and confess to Mr. Kingsley. He'll understand, and although he might be a little cross with you both, he'd never sack you, or anything like that.'

Jane had to smile, in spite of her dejection. How little these two knew! It would be interesting to repeat Scott's recent threat to dismiss both her and Les, just to note their reaction.

However, she merely said that as far as she was concerned nothing serious could come of the 'Hal business' as Susan had termed it.

'He's not my type,' she added, injecting a note of finality into her voice which both Susan and David noticed, and respected. But in any case, the conversation would have been interrupted owing to the unexpected appearance of Scott himself. Jane was the first to see his low white car gliding along the wide, palm-shaded avenue leading from the road to the hotel entrance, and her nerves tingled. For some indefinable reason she experienced a strange uneasiness at the idea of being in Scott's company and in that of Susan and David at the same time.

'Why, here's Mr. Kingsley!' There was no mistaking the pleasure in Susan's voice. 'How very nice!'

'I wonder what he wants?' David rose as the car came to rest under a rugged mahogany tree, and Scott slid his long body from the driver's seat. He stood for a second, staring at Jane, then flicked the car door closed.

'Good afternoon.' His greeting embraced them all and they responded. 'I'd like to have a word with you in private, Mr. Shore,' he added without preamble. 'It's about the projected extension.'

'Yes, Mr. Kingsley – of course. We can talk in my study.'

'They'll be there until tea time,' delared Susan with a grimace. 'Mr. Kingsley had said he might be away this week-end; he must have changed his mind.'

'Imagine his working on Sunday,' said Jane musingly, her eyes following the two men as they disappeared into the hotel. 'I'd no idea he'd do that.'

'He seems to work very hard. I suppose, being single, he hasn't much else to do. He's bought that lovely house, but I don't think he has much home life. Men on their own seldom do have. Mr. Kingsley always reminds me of a man who ought to be married, with a wife whose chief interests are him, his children, and his home – in that order.' A small laugh followed, and as Susan's gaze was on the view over the hotel gardens to the shore below, she missed Jane's shadowed expression, reflecting the deep regret which even once again encompassed her.

# CHAPTER EIGHT

IT was half past four when the two men emerged from the hotel to join the girls on the lawn. Jane and Susan had been playing tennis, Susan having lent Jane a pair of white shorts, which Jane still wore and which flatteringly revealed her shapely brown thighs. Scott's glance flickered over her before coming to rest on her face. She was relaxing on a garden chair after her strenuous game and she felt hot and knew her hair was awry. Her thoughts flew to Alma, always so immaculate, and Jane thought that Scott must surely be making comparisons. But on noting the indifference which had taken place of the slight interest of a few seconds ago she decided he was not sufficiently interested to be making comparisons.

'Had a good game?' he addressed Susan rather than Jane, and she nodded and smiled.

'Very good, thank you, Mr. Kingsley. Jane plays a wonderful game.'

'She does?' That flickering glance again. 'I must have a game with her myself, then.'

'Oh, no—!' exclaimed Jane involuntarily. 'I wouldn't play with you.'

'Why not?' with a slant of his eyebrows. 'I'm a player of very indifferent skill, I assure you.'

She was sure he lied and said without thinking,

'I rather think you would be bored by playing with me.'

'By playing . . .?' with a subtle inflection and a

shadow of a smile. He appeared to forget the two others present as he added, 'I assure you, my dear Jane, that playing with you would afford me immense pleasure.'

David and Susan exchanged swift glances. Jane went red, and flashed a furious look at her employer. To her utter relief the situation was eased by David's remarking that Mr. Kingsley would have his little joke. It was a weak effort, but Jane was grateful to David for all that. She wondered what he and Susan were thinking. It was bad enough for Scott to have used her Christian name, without his subtle tones and faint but unmistakable stress on the final two words.

'We can play all together,' submitted Susan, rather tentatively, but Scott ignored this and Jane saw at once that his silence had put Susan in her place as his employee.

'Will you stay to tea?' asked David, but Scott shook his head.

'I must go. I'll see you again early in the week about a start being made on the additions. The chalets can be erected without any interference to the smooth running of the hotel. We'll leave the alterations to the main building until the end of the season.'

David nodded. Clearly he was very happy at the vast improvements which were to be made.

'I think it's an excellent idea to have the chalets. Families can have complete freedom and privacy and yet enjoy all the facilities of the hotel, including the restaurant.'

Scott nodded, mechanically, his attention now being wholly on Jane. He said at length as if coming to a sudden decision,

'You can come along with me, Jane. I have things to discuss with you as well.'

'Me?' She stared, acutely conscious of the astonishment of her friends at this unexpected request. Request? It was an order, as the expression in Scott's eyes fully revealed. 'I have my car here.'

'It can be left. I'll send someone over in the morning to collect it and deliver it to Coral Gables.' Jane made no immediate move and he said brusquely, 'If you'll go now and change . . .?

She rose at once, recalling her tinge of uneasiness on Scott's arrival. Unconsciously she must have known he would say something to embarrass her.

When she came back from Susan's bedroom, where she had changed into her own clothes, Scott and David were standing by Scott's car, while Susan came slowly towards Jane, meeting her by a glorious bed of tropical shrubs which had been recently made to embellish the part of the lawn nearest to the hotel, a great curve having been cut out of the lawn to accommodate the additional bed. Deep red Chinese hibiscus flared in the sun; morning glory and golden shower and the brilliant flame vine contributed to the breathtaking beauty of the new addition to the already spectacular attractions of the grounds of the hotel. Above, balconies dripped with trailing vines, and palms waved everywhere against the blue of the Caribbean sky. Below, the coast of Bathsheba curved between the rocky spurs, and long white breakers spumed against the shore. Away on the landward skyline the sails of a windmill broke against the vivid blue, rising from the grounds of some plantation house among the surrounding acres of bright green sugar canes.

'Wasn't Mr. Kingsley strange?' Susan spoke a trifle hesitantly, for she had grasped that there was something unusual in the relationship existing between Jane and her employer. 'Imagine his wanting you today – Sunday. Surely he isn't expecting you to go do some work?'

Clearly Susan was pumping, but Jane forgave her, fully understanding her curiosity.

'I haven't any idea what he wants me for,' she replied frankly.

'To tell you to leave your car like that,' went on Susan. 'How will you get to Driftwood House in the morning?'

'I can take the hotel taxi.'

'Yes . . . I suppose you can—'

'Jane!' The call was abrupt and commanding. 'I'm waiting for you.'

Jane actually found herself running towards the car.

'I'm sorry,' she began, when Scott interrupted her.

'I don't expect my employees to keep me waiting. Get into the car!' So imperious now that voice, and his eyes were hard as metal. But his whole manner changed as he turned once more to David. 'It's been a most satisfactory afternoon.' He smiled at Susan, who had just come up. 'Goodbye, Mrs. Shore,' and with a nod to David he slid into his seat and within seconds the car was purring along the avenue towards the road.

Jane said quiveringly after a while,

'Your attitude towards me has set the Shores wondering.'

'Wondering? What about?'

'Well . . . as to the reason why you should be so – so sharp with me.' Quite without being conscious of it Jane allowed her voice to catch, and Scott turned swiftly to look at her. For a long moment he hesitated and then, just as abruptly as before,

'You kept me waiting. I had every right to be sharp with you. When I give an employee of mine an order I expect it to be obeyed immediately. You not only took your time over changing but you also stopped to gossip to your friend, knowing full well that I was waiting.'

'I didn't think. In any case, it *is* Sunday, and I was on a social visit to my friends.'

'I require your services. You can have an hour or two off another day.'

Jane said quietly,

'I have to do something for you?'

'Of course.'

'But,' she murmured after a small pause, 'we aren't going to your house.'

Again his head twisted and he regarded her profile.

'And what makes you say that?'

'This isn't the right direction.'

He smiled an odd little smile and said in a quizzical tone,

'You're not afraid I might be carrying you off to some lonely place with the intention of – er – forcing my attentions upon you?'

Jane coloured.

'Are we going to do some work or aren't we?'

'Careful, Jane,' he warned softly. 'No impertinence. You will keep forgetting that I'm your employer.'

'I can scarcely forget that,' she retorted, 'when you come along and order me to leave my friends and accompany you to – I don't know where!'

'Order?' He mused on this for a space. 'I shouldn't have thought you'd mind in the least. After all, you're one of those women who enjoy being ordered about.'

'I certainly am not!'

One eyebrow slanted.

'But you gave me to believe that you did.'

'I? When?'

'A long time ago, my dear. Surely you haven't changed? You do still want a tyrant for a husband ... when the time comes for you to marry?'

'I never said I wanted a tyrant for a husband.'

'Not in so many words—' He broke off and swerved as a taxi carrying tourists came racing round a bend. 'Charlie,' he murmured, 'telling jokes as usual and not looking where he's going.' The native driver had been roaring with laughter and so had his fares. 'As I was saying,' continued Scott when once they had the road to themselves again, a road running through endless acres of sugar canes, 'you never actually said it, but you meant it. A master, you wanted, tyrannical and iron-handed—'

'I did not want that kind of a man!' she broke in furiously. 'I merely wanted someone who wouldn't give in to me at every turn.'

'I should think there are few men who would do that,' he commented after a little thoughtful silence, as if he were in the process of recollection. 'He wouldn't be a man if he did.'

Jane gave a small sigh and asked where they were going.

'Changing the subject, eh? Cowardly Jane,' he jeered. 'Where are we going? I'm taking you out to tea. Do you mind?'

'To tea?' she gasped, her heart jerking in the most delicious way.

'Need you exhibit such astonishment? We're only going to Sam Lord's Castle, not to the moon.'

'Sam Lord's?'

'Would you like to go somewhere else?'

'I hadn't thought of going anywhere. You said you had some work for me to do.'

'I don't recollect saying any such thing. I said I had things to discuss with you.'

'I took it for granted that it appertained to work.'

Scott ignored this and asked again if she would care to go somewhere else for tea.

'No,' she said obligingly, 'Sam Lord's will be very nice.'

'So there's no argument,' to himself, and she knew instinctively that he was recalling the time when she had deliberately set out to overrule him. And he had hoped she would make a similar endeavour now – when he would promptly have told her she was going to the place he had chosen. Well, she thought with some considerable satisfaction, she hadn't given him the chance of flaunting his authority over her.

They were travelling south-east and on their right rose the spectacular height of Hackleton's Cliff, while to the left the windward coast spread towards the great expanse of blue sea and the horizon which merged hazily into it. From the parish of St. John they entered that of St. Philip and were soon driving towards the castellated Regency house situated in a dramatic tropical setting on the south-east coast of the island where the incessant roaring of the surf provided background music to the almost theatrical atmosphere of the dignified and imposing house which had such an interesting place in the history of the island, being the one-time stronghold of the infamous buccaneer Sam Lord who, with his gang of cut-throats, looted ships and murdered their crews after having lured them to the reefs by hanging lanterns in the trees, lanterns which when swinging in the breeze looked like lights on ships safely at anchor.

Scott was known at the castle, now a modern luxury hotel, and he and Jane were shown to a table in a secluded corner with a view to the exotic gardens and the wooded region beyond.

'You haven't expressed much surprise at my request that you should take tea with me.' Scott was in a most attractive mood all at once as, leaning back in his chair he looked across at her with an expression half amused, half admiring in his eyes.

'Request?' she repeated sweetly, allowing a hint of humour to enter her own eyes.

He laughed.

'Now what do you want me to say to that, I wonder?'

'Admit that it was an order.'

He inclined his head.

'All right, it was.'

'And the reason for it?' Jane was happy, talking in this light vein to Scott. It reminded her of the man she had known long ago, the man with whom she so often talked in this manner. At that time he was more free and spontaneous, having no responsibilities of business as he had now. And he had been young for his age; he was young again, but not quite in the same way. Beneath this youthful exterior lay the unmistakable fact of his maturity and of his concern with the business of making money.

'I desired company.'

Jane was reminded of what Susan had said about his not having much home life. He ought to have a wife, Susan had asserted – a wife whose chief interests would be him, his children and his home . . .

Was he lonely? wondered Jane, and a shadow crossed her lovely face at the idea. Yet it was the life he had chosen, she instantly went on to remind herself. He could have been married long ago had he wished.

She said rather timidly at last,

'My company?'

'Yes, Jane; your company.'

She swallowed the little lump rising in her throat. Happy as she was there was still present the regret for what she had lost – no, not lost, but thrown away, deliberately and without even stopping to think that the day might dawn when she would suddenly wake up to the fact that she would give anything to retrieve what she had so carelessly cast away.

'Here's the waiter,' she stammered awkwardly, quite unable to find anything to say in response to his quietly-spoken admission. 'We'd better be – be looking at – at the menu.'

He had been gazing at her with a half grave, half amused expression and at her loss of composure a suspended smile broke, dispelling the gravity and strengthening the humour.

'I merely wanted a sandwich or two and a cup of

tea.'

'Is that all?'

'You must have more. I'm sure you're hungry after your game of tennis.'

The native waiter was smiling by the table, revealing a row of strong white teeth.

'Sandwiches for me—' Scott flicked a hand towards Jane. 'The lady wants something more. Bring some of your delicious confections.'

They ate and drank tea and chatted, then strolled in the beautiful grounds of the hotel which went down to one of the loveliest beaches in the Caribbean.

'I ought to be getting back,' sighed Jane at last, her reluctance plainly revealed in her expression and her tone. 'Les will be wondering where I am.'

Was it imagination or had a frown appeared fleetingly on Scott's brow?

'We'll go back to Driftwood House and telephone him from there – unless you'd prefer to ring him from here?'

She looked swiftly at him, puzzled.

'Why should we go back to your house?'

'For no especial reason.'

Nonplussed, she could find nothing to say for a full minute and they continued to stroll among the flowers.

'Les will expect me to be back for dinner,' she managed at last.

'That's a long time off.' He glanced down at her, eyes flickering over her face and hair and figure. 'In fact, you can have dinner with me.'

Silence. It was a tense moment, full of strange vibrations, deep and yet impalpable. Every nerve in

Jane's body seemed alive to the profundity of the situation as she and Scott stood very still in the quiet beauty of the tropical gardens, the balmy breeze from the blue ocean caressing their faces.

Jane tried to make her voice light and half jesting, but wondered if she succeeded in hiding from Scott the fact that her emotions were heightened, her nerves tensed.

'Is this another order?'

'It could be.'

'I might decide to disobey it.'

'But I could enforce it.'

'You could?' with sudden curiosity. 'How?'

At that a hint of satirical amusement touched the corners of his mouth. The blue eyes came alive, as Jane had seen them come alive in the past.

'Now, dear Jane, you're obviously asking for a demonstration, and this I can't give you until I have you at home . . . at my mercy.'

The colour fluctuated in her cheeks; she had no idea just how appealing she was at this moment, with her big hazel eyes raised to his and her fingers locking and unlocking in a little nervous gesture of which she was wholly unconscious. Once again she attempted to assume a buoyant veneer as she said,

'Your threats don't frighten me. I can hold my own.'

He raised his eyebrows.

'Is that a challenge?' he queried with mock surprise.

'It could be,' she replied, borrowing his own phrase of a moment ago.

'Ah . . . In that case, let's go home without further

delay.'

Jane laughed then, and it was a gay laugh such as she had not given for a long time. Scott's deep-set eyes fixed themselves on her face and he seemed for one astounding moment to be lost for words.

It was Jane who broke the silence, presently saying,

'What will you do if I refuse to go to your home?'

'You forget, my dear,' was his rather dry rejoinder, 'that I have a hold over you.'

'You'd force me to accompany you to your home?'

'Without a doubt I would.' He paused, but she waited for him to continue. 'You don't appear too apprehensive at the idea of my forcing you to come home with me?'

'I've been there many times already,' she reminded him.

'As my secretary. It's not as my secretary that I'm taking you home today.'

At this she forgot her light veneer and said, her eyes searching his face with a hint of anxiety in their depths,

'Are you really quite serious about my coming to your home today?'

'I thought I'd made it clear that I was serious.'

'You want me to dine with you?'

'Correct.'

'I'm not dressed for dining out.'

'We're not dining out.'

Jane began shaking her head, recalling vividly the way he had forced his kisses on her and affirmed that they would find pleasure together. The way she felt today she was not at all sure she could put up a strong enough resistance should he decide once again to take her in his arms and tempt her. Deeply aware of her love for him, she decided that caution should overrule her more emotional temptation to accept his invitation and spend the evening at Driftwood House. The lush tropical setting in which the house stood was in itself a danger, being too romantic by far.

'I must go back to Coral Gables,' she said at last.

He looked questioningly at her.

'I thought it was settled that we dined at my home?'

'No . . . I must go back to Coral Gables,' she repeated, a note of desperation creeping into her voice.

Emphatically Scott shook his head, an implacable expression on his face.

'I've just said I'd force you to dine with me,' he reminded her.

'You were joking, surely?'

'No such thing. I was never more serious.' He began walking on again and she fell in beside him. They reached the car park and Jane hesitated.

'I ought to go home—'

'My dear girl,' he broke in with some asperity, 'get in and let's have no more fuss!'

She obeyed, and it was only when they were on their way that she managed to speak, and even then it was only to say, rather feebly, that she should have telephoned her brother.

'Do it from my house,' he said abruptly, and a silence once again fell between them. What was his object? she wondered, casting him a sidelong glance and noting the firm set profile, the bronzed skin and attractive brown hair, thick and shining as if it had only that moment been vigorously brushed.

'Relax,' he told her eventually, 'and enjoy the drive. I'm going the long way round.' He flicked her a glance and she saw his sudden smile, that spontaneous smile which set her heart racing in spite of her efforts at control. 'You've viewed the scenery before, I expect but you'll appreciate it just the same.'

His tone had lost its austere edge and Jane received the impression that he had almost allowed an element of gentleness to creep into it. She realized, not for the first time, that there were still remnants of the old Scott in his present make-up, alhough he invariably suppressed them.

He drove back towards the windward coast and the rugged Bathsheba shoreline, more picturesque than ever in the early evening sunlight. Continuing along the east coast road he eventually cut across the island, passing through the rugged Scotland District and down the west coast, passing hotels with glamorous names like Sunset Lodge and Buccaneer Bay and Coconut Creek, each of which stood in exotic grounds with waving palms and magnificent views.

At last they were at Driftwood House, and the car was brought smoothly to a halt at the front door. Polly opened it before Scott could use his key. She produced her customary broad smile and listened while Scott told her that he had brought a guest for dinner.

'We will have something special,' she promised, and went away, in the direction of the kitchen.

## CHAPTER NINE

THE very excellent dinner was served in the high-ceilinged dining-room where tapestries adorned the walls and the furniture was old and mellowed. Candles lighted the table where gleamed silver plate and cutlery set on an exquisitely-embroidered tablecloth. A Derby dinner service completed a picture of luxury and gracious living, while the meal itself was the most delicious Jane had ever eaten. It included the exotic flying fish and other Bajan dishes, with several kinds of fruit to follow. Coffee and liqueurs were served on the verandah which was also lit by candles, put there merely for effect and perhaps to supplement the moonlight a little.

Scott reclined against a cushion and watched Jane as she sipped her drink.

'I hope you've enjoyed the meal,' he said, breaking the long silence at last.

'It was lovely, thank you.'

'Glad you agreed to dine here?' An eyebrow slanted; he had a teasing expression in those vivid blue eyes.

'If you remember,' she replied in a quiet measured tone, 'I had no choice.'

The half-smile hovering on his lips was traded for a laugh.

'But you enjoyed having the choice made for you?'

'I'm glad I came,' she admitted. 'That's what you want me to say, isn't it?'

'Only if it's true.'

'It is,' she responded quietly, and lifted her cup to her lips, bending her head so as to conceal her expression.

'We must do it again,' he decided.

Jane hesitated before speaking, not because she had any fault to find with Scott's suggestion, but owing to the fact that Les was not in possession of the knowledge that Scott knew the truth – that Les was her brother and not her husband.

'Les will consider it most strange that you should take me off. When I phoned him saying I was coming here for the evening he sounded puzzled.' She glanced at Scott, inviting some comment, but he merely waited for her to continue, a quizzical expression on his face. 'You must remember that he's still under the impression that you believe us to be husband and wife. He wouldn't expect you to be taking me away from him – taking his wife away, I mean—' She broke off as a dry laugh broke from her companion's lips.

'I wonder,' he said reflectively, 'if you ever stopped to think about the muddle you might find yourself in?'

'I didn't like the idea of the deceit at all, and I did wonder if it would result in trouble for us.'

'But of course, you couldn't visualize just how much trouble it might cause.'

'I never expected to find you here,' she said with feeling.

'And if you had?'

'Then most certainly I wouldn't have agreed to the plan at all.'

He considered this and a frown appeared on his brow.

'Fate is strange,' he murmured almost to himself. 'I never expected ever to see you again . . .' He stopped, slowly, and lost himself in thought. Jane was shut out, but she did speculate on his strange manner, and, quite unbidden, hope leapt high within her. Was it possible that he still cared? Surely not – after all this time. Besides, he had declared quite emphatically that marriage was not for him. Yet the next moment Jane was recalling once again Susan's suggestion that he worked because he lacked any real home life. She also recalled her own idea that he was lonely. He had no need to be lonely, though. On his own admission he'd had many women, so obviously he could have many more. Where was Alma? Scott could have gone over to St. Vincent, surely, and spent the week-end with her – unless of course she was with her other boy-friend.

'I think it's time I was getting back,' she said when there was no sign of his breaking the silence. 'If you insist that I keep my brother in the dark about your knowing the true position then I must act the part accordingly. He'll ask me awkward questions as it is.'

Scott came from his contemplative mood and shrugged his shoulders.

'He'll merely conclude that I'm one of those employers who have no principles. I wouldn't be unique, by any means.'

'He has a very high opinion of you.'

'Indeed? Even though I've already shown my interest in you?'

'Interest,' she repeated a trifle breathlessly, her eyes seeking his with swift inquiry, an unusual brightness in their depths. 'You're interested in me?'

Scott regarded her intently and seemed filled with

some unfathomable indecision. But suddenly he had adopted his more customary air of cynicism and his voice was edged with satire as he said,

'But of course, my dear Jane. You know full well I'm interested in you. Haven't I invited you to have an affair with me?'

Jane's heart sank. She would have done anything to take back the eager question that had resulted in this change in his manner.

'I've no intention of having an affair with you,' she retorted, dejection breeding anger. It seemed impossible that only a few moments ago she had allowed hope to enter into her. Scott was a rake, and the sooner she accepted this the better.

He was looking speculatively at her.

'Don't be too sure, my dear,' he advised at length. 'If I really try, you'll not be able to resist me.'

Her eyes blazed.

'What an opinion you have of yourself!'

'You've said that before. Can't you think of anything more original?'

Jane finished her coffee. Anger surged, but she felt drained as well.

'I think I'll go,' she said dispiritedly, and rose to her feet.

He glanced at his watch.

'It's early,' he said, but eased himself out of his chair.

'It'll be ten by the time I get home.'

Scott shrugged.

'Very well. I'll take you.'

But, on their way to the car, he stopped and took her in his arms.

'Just one good night kiss,' he said, and bent his head.

'No – I—' the rest was smothered as his lips met hers.

'Delightful.' He held her from him, mockery in his gaze. 'How you do protest, Jane – and you don't mean it.'

She said flatly,

'I shan't argue with you, Scott. Perhaps, now you've had what you want, you'll be kind enough to take me home?'

'What I want?' he laughed. 'Dear Jane, I want much more from you than kisses!'

She felt her colour rise.

'Are we to go through all that again?'

'Perhaps,' he mused, ignoring her question, 'I should take what I want. After all, you should enjoy the love experience all the more for having been forced into it.' His hands slid to her waist, which he held tightly as she began to struggle. 'Shall I take you?' he whispered close to her cheek. 'I can, you know. You're completely at my mercy.'

She was frightened all at once, for it did seem that he was in a mood to carry out his threat. His warm breath caressed her cheek; his body, hard against her as his arms once again brought her to him, was masterfully demanding. Struggling in earnest, Jane ended by pleading and when this had no effect she started to cry. This alone sobered him and his ardency was checked.

He held her at arm's length, regarding her tear-filled eyes intently.

'All right,' he said abruptly, 'I'll take you home.'

When Jane arrived for work the following morning Scott's manner was such that the incident of the previous evening might never have happened. He was the employer, cool, indifferent. He never even seemed to notice her heightened colour when first she entered his room to take a letter. His voice was impassive, his face an expressionless mask.

Jane accepted him as he happened to be at any particular time and decided that from now on she would never for a second forget that she was his employee, and would act accordingly.

He was going to St. Vincent at the week-end, he told her later, but added that she would be expected to come in as there was a long report to do, a report appertaining to his plans for an extension to the Carib Palm Hotel.

'I'll expect it to be finished when I return on Sunday night,' he said.

'It'll be finished,' she told him stiffly, and as it was five o'clock she said goodbye and left his room.

Her car had been sent for and was at the end of the drive. She slid into her seat and pressed the starter. There was no response and she pressed it again. What was wrong with it? she wondered frowningly. Scott was at his window watching her, and at last she got out and looked over to where he was, having already stepped out on to the verandah.

'What's wrong?' he asked.

'It won't start,' she told him unnecessarily.

'Have you had trouble with it before?'

She shook her head.

'Not up till now, but then I haven't had it very long.'

'My man drove it here from Bathsheba; it was all right when he left it.' Scott moved the seat back and got in. A moment later he was looking at her in some amusement. 'Petrol,' he said. 'Cars usually go better when there's some in the tank.'

'There's none in?' she asked, and he shook his head.

'You look surprised. Did you think you had plenty?'

'Well . . . I hadn't really thought about it . . .' She tailed off as Scott shook his head in a faint gesture of disgust.

'How like a woman – not to bother about so vital a matter as petrol. Do you realize you might have been stranded on the road?'

'Yes. It was fortunate that I wasn't.'

'I'll take you home,' he offered. 'And I'll pick up a can of petrol on my way back. You can use the taxi to come to work in the morning.'

Les was standing outside the hotel talking to a couple of guests and he turned in surprise on seeing Scott's car arriving.

'Something wrong?' he asked anxiously as Scott and Jane got out of the car.

'Your – wife forgot to get any petrol in her car,' Scott's amused glance caught Jane's eye as he made the deliberate hesitation, 'so I had to bring her home.'

Les looked oddly at him and said,

'If you'd rung I'd have brought some petrol over.'

'It wasn't worth troubling you,' returned Scott carelessly. 'If you happen to have a can handy I'll take it. I don't have one myself . . . there being no necessity for it.' His eyes went to Jane again. Forgetting her gratitude, she sent him a speaking glance.

'Meaning that you could never possibly run out of petrol,' she flashed before she could stop herself. Les stared, as well he might, because in addition to Jane's anger and the apparent disrespect she was showing to their employer, Scott himself was acting in a rather peculiar manner, not only in the satire of his glance at Jane but also in the mocking inflection of his tone.

'I'll get someone to look for a can,' said Les, and went away.

Jane looked up at Scott and said belligerently,

'What are you trying to do? You've got Les really suspicious now!'

The blue eyes narrowed, and so did the smile that had hovered rather good-humouredly on his lips.

'How many times,' he asked, 'must I remind you that I'm your boss?'

'Employer!'

'Choose your own name. You'll still respect me – or else!'

'I'm getting a little tired of your threats, Scott. What exactly can you do?'

'Sack you both – send you back to England.'

This subdued her, as he meant it to. She muttered an apology, and added a thank-you for his bringing her home.

'No trouble,' he returned laconically, and turned to meet her brother, who had a gallon-sized can in his hand. 'Thanks,' he said, and with a nod to Jane he got into his car and drove off between the double row of trees that lined the path leading to the gate.

'Something strange going on,' muttered Les, turning to Jane. 'What was going on between you two was very much like the aftermath of a lovers' quarrel.'

'No such thing. I disliked his sarcasm, that's all, so I answered him back.'

'Forgetting that he's your employer?'

'I can never forget that,' she snapped, out of patience with Les as much as Scott. 'He's always reminding me of it.'

'He is?'

Only now did Jane realize that she had once again forgotten to be tactful.

'If I answer him back he reminds me, yes.'

Les shook his head thoughtfully.

'It's a funny set-up altogether,' he said tersely, and added, 'The bomb's going to explode shortly; I can see it coming!'

'What do you mean?'

'Scott'll have to be told the truth.'

'That we're not husband and wife?'

'Exactly.'

Jane looked curiously at him.

'Any particular reason for saying that?'

'Two reasons!'

'Oh?'

'First – you and Scott. It's no use your denying it, Jane, there's something going on between you that I don't know of. It's my belief that he'd be very happy to learn that you're free; and as for you yourself – I'm damned sure you're not as indifferent to him as you'd have me believe.'

She made no attempt to deny this.

'And the second reason?' she queried, slanting him a glance.

He hesitated a long while, a frown darkening his

brow.

'It's Gwen,' he said at length.

'Gwen? You – like her?'

He nodded.

'I more than like her, Jane.'

Jane said quietly,

'I'm glad, Les—No, don't interrupt to tell me you're not sure about your feelings being reciprocated. I happen to know that Gwen cares for you.'

His eyes opened wide.

'You do?' Troubled as he obviously was regarding the deceit which had been practised, he was also plainly relieved to know that he had a chance with Gwen. 'How?'

'I overheard her saying she must leave because of you. She believed she'd fallen in love with a married man.'

'You overheard this, and yet you never mentioned it?'

'It wasn't the thing one does mention.'

'But it would have put my mind at rest.'

'How did I know you cared? You've cared for some time?' she added as the thought occurred to her.

'For some time,' he owned. 'You knew she cared, that day when I asked if you'd any ideas as to the reason for her giving in her notice?'

'Yes, I did.'

'Well, it was a rotten trick not to tell me!'

'I wasn't in a position to tell you. I had no idea you'd be willing to open up and confess all to Scott.' It was suddenly borne in on Jane that once Les made his confession she herself would be freed from the hold Scott had on her, and of which he was so fond of reminding her.

'I've been through hell,' Les confessed, ignoring her protest. 'I asked you if you had any ideas why she was leaving,' he repeated. 'I hated the thought of her going.'

'Then why didn't you give her some clue that you cared?' Jane spoke crossly, feeling she was being maltreated at every turn. As soon as Les's confession was made she would go home, she decided.

'How could I when she believed me to be married?'

Jane shrugged exasperatedly.

'Don't look at me as if I'm to blame. It was your idea to pretend we were man and wife.'

'I'm sorry, Jane,' he said in a much softer tone. 'I'm in such a devil of a mess – oh, I know you had doubts right from the first that all wouldn't go smoothly, but that's not important now. What is important is that Gwen must be prevented from leaving Coral Gables. I don't want to be put to the trouble of going to England after her.'

'You'd do that?' Jane had to smile to herself, for Les's expression had never been more harassed.

'Certainly I would.' A pause and then, 'Have you any idea as to how Scott will take the news of our deception?'

Carelessly she shrugged. But this new deception was almost as worrying to her as the other. She felt she ought to be frank with Les at once, but she was ever conscious of Scott's order that she must keep silent.

'I haven't, Les. But Susan and David seem to think Scott won't be too angry about it.'

'Susan and Dave? How come they to be discussing

the possibility of our making a confession?'

'They were joking about Hal Charlton – I told you I met him at the Yacht Club dance?' Les nodded and Jane went on to repeat what Susan had said about the probability of the secret having to come out. 'They seemed to think that you also would eventually want to let it be known that you aren't married.'

Les nodded and went on to tell Jane that, one afternoon when David called, he had said, on noticing how Les was with Gwen,

'Nice girl. You seem fond of her?'

'He did?' Jane was nodding absently. 'So he and Susan must then have drawn their own conclusions – that you'd be driven to tell Scott the truth.'

'It appears so.' Les looked curiously at her. 'This Hal – he doesn't mean a thing to you, I take it?'

She started to shake her head, then gave him a puzzled glance.

'Why are you so sure?'

Les slanted an eyebrow.

'Because, Jane, no matter how much you try to deny it, there's only one man in your life.' She merely blushed and he went on, 'You made no protest just now when I said that there's something going on between you that I don't know of, and that he'd be happy to learn that you're my sister and not my wife.'

She did speak then, to reiterate her statement that Scott was not now interested in her, and that he certainly wasn't interested in marriage.

'He says he can have all the fun without it,' she added in a tone suddenly gone flat. 'Besides, there's Alma.'

'A mere plaything,' shrugged Les.

'Scott used to be such a moral, honourable man,' she mused with a pained expression that was not lost on her observant brother.

'Until you chucked him, eh? Pride with a man like Scott's important; he must have hated you for what you did.'

Jane nodded forlornly.

'I expect so,' she admitted.

Les stared absently at the cascading showers of the golden cassia bush which grew to one side of the imposing entrance to the hotel.

'I can't agree, though, that he isn't interested in you once again. You've only got to think about his conduct. First, he took you as his secretary—'

'That was natural. He knew I could do the work, and as there wasn't anyone else available he gave me the job. It was entirely for his own convenience.'

Ignoring that, Les asked bluntly,

'Wouldn't you like to believe there was some other reason for his taking you as his secretary?'

She hesitated, then decided that her brother had already guessed too much for a dishonest answer to be remotely effective.

'Yes, Les, I would like to think there was some other reason . . . but there wasn't,' she added, a catch in her voice.

'I reckon we'll just have to wait and see,' was all Les proffered, and the subject was dropped.

True to his word Hal followed up his intention of seeing more of Jane and he came to dine and dance one evening when there was a special entertainment on at Coral Gables. A famous steel band and calypso singers had been engaged, and two equally famous limbo dancers. The performances took place outside, amid flowers and palms and exotic perfumes drifting on the gentle zephyr blowing in from the north-east – the welcome cooling trade wind breeze. As always the tables were set around the area where the entertainments and dancing were to take place. Candles flickered from their coloured jars, throwing off subdued, romantic light. All around, among the palms, tall lamps gave off an added illumination, their naked flares dancing with the breeze. The tropical scene was set for a typical Caribbean evening of dining, dancing and a superb floor show performed entirely by natives. The steel band musicians were attired in gaily-coloured shorts and trousers, their instruments were painted in dazzling colours also. Away from the actual precincts of the hotel the palm-fringed private beach shone in the moonlight, lapped by the gentle Caribbean Sea.

In this exotic setting Jane and Hal dined and danced, watched the floor show and danced again. Half-way through the evening Scott walked in, alone, and glanced all around, his eyes at last finding what they sought. With his customary easy languid strides he was soon dispensing with the distance between him and the table at which Jane and Hal sat.

'Good evening, Jane – Hal.'

'Good evening. Care to join us?' Hal's invitation was half-hearted, to say the least, and Scott regarded him with sudden hauteur.

'Yes, I would,' he replied, eyes flitting to Jane who was moving her chair round a little in order to make room for the extra chair to be brought to the tiny table.

Scott sat down and for a few minutes they all

watched the limbo dance. It was performed with the legs wide open and, Jane had learned, was originally a love dance brought to the island by slaves from Africa. The men moved their bodies with grace and rhythm, easing themselves under the long bar that was very close to the ground.

Scott asked what Jane and Hal were drinking and ordered; Les came and joined them, managing to squeeze in another chair. He drank one of the many ambrosial concoctions based on the island's splendid rum.

When the limbo dance was over Scott stood up, inviting Jane to dance. She caught the amused glance of her brother and also Hal's swift frown as she slipped into the arms of her employer.

'You appear to have forgotten my order,' he said crisply once they were away from the table, and occupying part of the space on which the floor show had been performed.

'Order?' she flashed.

'I told you to act in a more seemly manner where Hal Charlton was concerned.'

'And what have I done?' she demanded curtly.

'You were sitting with him at a table for two. And until you saw me you had your heads practically touching – like lovers.'

Jane felt his fingers on her back; they dug in like rods of iron.

'That's not true,' she denied with reserve and dignity. 'We were chatting, and as there was noise going on all around we had to be close.'

'You're supposed to be married! If any man should have been sitting with you it should have been Les.'

'He was busy.'

'You said you liked this fellow Hal Charlton. Was that the truth?'

She paused, but fleetingly.

'Yes, it was.' If he could be convinced, she thought, it would put an end once and for all to his amorous approaches.

'I see.' The two small words were bitten out and the blue eyes were cold and hard as steel. 'You don't care that he has a reputation?'

'Most men have,' she shrugged, and added as the thought occurred to her, 'You yourself have said more than once that it doesn't matter any more. People don't have ideals.'

'But you do – or so you told me,' he reminded her tersely.

'I'm not saying I'll go as far as marrying Hal,' she said, and again felt the hard fingers press into her back.

'You can't – as things are,' he reminded her tautly.

'No . . .' Should she inform him that he could expect a confession from her brother very soon? It would be enjoyable to watch his reaction, to remind him – just in case the fact had not occurred to him – that he would no longer be in a position to impose his will upon her, since his hold over her would be removed. However, the confession being entirely Les's affair, Jane held her tongue, but she did say, veering the subject a little, 'If you're thinking of anything so authoritative as forbidding me to see Hal, then I wouldn't if I were you. I'm becoming a little tired of being ordered about.'

His brows lifted, not with arrogance but surprise,

although Jane suspected this was assumed.

'You amaze me,' he mocked. 'Obviously some change has taken place. I seem to remember—'

'Oh, please!' she snapped irritably. 'Forget all that nonsense—'

'So it was nonsense,' he cut in swiftly, a curious expression in his eyes. 'You admit it – after all this time?'

'I don't want to be domineered and ordered about – no woman in her right mind does!'

'All right, all right,' soothingly as, with a hand beneath her elbow, he guided her away from the noisy throng, towards the pale golden shore. 'There's no need to go into hysterics over it.'

'I'm not in hysterics!'

'You'll not deny you're in a foul temper, though?' His mocking glance changed to one of amusement. 'You're an over-emotional girl, Jane. Whoever takes you on for a wife is in for the very devil of a time . . . unless,' he added with a sort of dry humour, 'he has the sense to beat you right at the start.' He laughed at her anger and infuriated her even more by patting one bright red cheek. 'I should have done, I'm thinking – once I'd discovered this side of your nature.'

She could have said no, he wouldn't, as at that time his only aim was to pander and please. But of course she remained silent, not only because she had no wish to pursue a topic which was embarrassing for her but also because she was now not at all sure that he was any less without strength of character four years ago than he was now. Les had maintained that Scott had loved her so much that he had let her have all her own way, and this Jane was very much inclined to accept.

Scott was walking on, making her go with him as his hand was kept under her elbow. The night was magical, the tropical moon high and bright, like polished silver; and the stars, lustrous and scintillating, streaked across the deep midnight blue of the Caribbean sky. Music and perfume floated through the soft warm air.

The atmosphere was suddenly overpowering, the man by her side projecting his personality without conscious effort, or even knowledge. Jane felt as if she were to be caught in a web woven by all the magical threads of nature but held invitingly open by the man at her side.

'I want to go back,' she said impulsively just as Scott decided to halt under the very same coconut palm where their first meeting in Barbados had taken place. 'Take – take me back!'

He stared, then laughed, deriving amusement from the fear in her eyes.

'Rather a belated request, isn't it?'

'I – wasn't looking wh-where we were going.'

'Not a soul anywhere . . . just you and me and the sea and sky. It might be a desert island . . .' And before she could twist away in anticipation of what he intended she was caught to him and kissed with a passion so intense that she actually felt her senses leaving her. Never in the old days had he displayed ardour such as this. So gentle he had been, so afraid of hurting her, either mentally or physically. But not so now; his arms were hawsers, merciless, unyielding, his lips ruthlessly demanding, cruel in their possessiveness. After an eternity Scott held her from him, his eyes smouldering embers of desire, his voice vibrant and throaty. 'Thank your lucky stars we're not alone on a desert island, for if

we were then all those ideals of yours would be lost—'
he stopped and a low laugh escaped him '—along with
your virtue, my lovely, desirable Jane!'

## CHAPTER TEN

Utterly drained and with her heart beating over-rate, Jane managed to break away from the hands holding her.

'Don't run!' Scott caught her up in a second. 'You're going to look foolish, racing back like that.'

'And what are you going to look like?' she quivered, more shaken by her own emotions than by the effect of his.

'I should just leave you,' he replied smoothly, and she did wonder how he could have recovered his composure so swiftly. 'You'd go back on your own – and everyone would look askance, wondering what had got into you.'

'You're detestable! I shall be very glad when I'm free to go home, as I shall be soon—' Too late she broke off; her wrist was caught and she was swung round and brought roughly to a standstill.

'What did you say?' Soft tones but menacing. Jane felt as afraid of him in this mood as she had been a few minutes earlier. What a lot she had learned about Scott since coming to Barbados – Scott, the 'spineless jellyfish' that she had branded him. She could have laughed at the memory of her own derogatory opinion of him.

'It was nothing—'

'What did you say?' he broke in to repeat in the same dangerously quiet tone.

She was on the verge of tears, and blinked rapidly as

she looked up into his inscrutable countenance.

'You'll know soon enough—' Jane broke off and uttered a little cry of protest as, losing his patience, Scott gave her a shake.

'Now,' he said between his teeth, 'will you expand on what you were about to say?'

Defeated, she told him that Les was soon to make a full confession.

'He's fallen in love with Gwen, you see,' she added, a catch in her voice caused partly by suppressed tears and partly by her inner trembling as a result of the shaking he had given her.

'He wants to marry her?' he asked, for the moment diverted from the main issue.

'Yes, I expect so.'

'I see . . .' He became thoughtful; Jane wondered if he were realizing that his hold over her was about to be severed, and that from then on he would no longer be in a position to order her about. He would of course still be her employer – for as long as she decided to remain with him – but he would certainly not be able to treat her as he had treated her this evening. 'Has he considered just how difficult it's going to be for him to face everyone?'

'No, I don't believe he has.' She herself had not dwelt much on this aspect of the situation. Les had made a few friends on the island and it was going to be extremely awkward to confess to them that Jane was his sister and not his wife.

'He does know that I might sack him?'

Her heart contracted.

'He's prepared for this, I suppose, but we had begun to assume that your satisfaction with the way the hotel were being run—' She stopped, arrested by the widening of his eyes as an expression of inquiry replaced the previous unreadable quality in his gaze. 'I've done it again,' she added absurdly at length.

'Apparently you have. I'm extremely interested to know more. Your mention of hotels in the plural signifies that your friends, the Shores, are fairly confident I'll condone the deception?'

Reluctantly she admitted that this was so.

'We naturally talked about it one day,' she added, and as he appeared ready to lose his temper she decided to tell him all that had been said.

'So because I consider an employee of mine to be efficient I must overlook anything so serious as the deceit that's been practised,' he said grimly at last. 'Their confidence amazes me! I've a good mind to clear the whole lot of you out!'

'No – please don't,' she begged, on the point of tears. 'The Shores acted in all good faith when they recommended Les for the post. They believed him to be almost engaged to Carolyn – that was the girl he'd been keeping company with for some months.'

Scott was silent for a space after she had finished speaking. His mouth was set and his eyes implacable. Her heart sank as she visualized David and Susan losing their jobs because of what they had done for Les.

At last Scott spoke, to say he would have to think more about the whole matter, and perhaps discuss it with one or two other directors of the firm.

'Need you?' she cried. 'They won't find any extenuating circumstances at all.'

'What makes you think I shall?' he countered, looking coolly at her.

'You've seen what David and Susan – the Shores – have done. You must admit you've been very pleased with the way they've run the hotel?'

'I pay for efficiency,' he said abruptly. 'Therefore I expect it. The way you talk I should be grateful to the Shores!'

Swiftly she shook her head.

'No, I didn't mean it like that—' She stopped and shrugged helplessly. 'You're not in the mood to understand,' she added flatly at length.

'You're quite right; I'm not.' He looked at her in silence for a moment. 'What are your own plans?'

So the fact *had* hit him that she would soon be out of his power. Strangely, and for some quite incomprehensible reason, this failed to afford her the satisfaction she had expected.

'I thought of going home,' she told him quietly.

A deep ineffable hush fell, broken only by the gentle lapping of the sea on the curving shoreline.

'So you'd let me down?' he said at last in a very quiet tone.

'You would soon get someone to take my place.' Already she wished she had not said what she had. The thought of leaving and never seeing Scott again created a bleak picture indeed.

'You'd also leave Hal, whom you say you're fond of?' His eyes fixed hers now and she averted her head.

'The friendship hasn't ripened into anything that can't be broken,' she murmured.

'So you lied when you told me you cared for him?'

'I said liked. No, I didn't lie,' she was quick to add,

feeling that unless she used Hal she would surely give away her love for Scott.

'So you're determined to leave Barbados?'

She hesitated, then common sense intervened to remind her that to remain must bring further heartache – nothing more. True, she had at one point fell to wondering if she had a chance with Scott, and Les most certainly seemed convinced that she had. But if Scott wanted her for his wife he had only to say so; it was as simple as that. No, all he wanted was for her to be another Alma – a woman to have fun with, and then cast aside when a new and more attractive face caught his attention.

'Yes,' she managed at last. 'I'm determined to leave the island.'

'I see,' tautly and with a most formidable light in his eyes. 'Then there's nothing more to say. Come, let's get back. Your boy-friend will be wondering where you've got to.'

Les was troubled; he looked at his sister's shadowed face and said,

'You really feel that he'll sack David and Susan?'

'I can't say for sure,' she replied, frowning. 'I've told you everything that was said – or nearly everything. Scott was certainly angry about the whole deception – theirs as well as ours.'

'I don't know why you had to let it out like that! It was my affair entirely.'

'It came out by accident,' Jane said, repeating what she had already told him. She was having the greatest difficulty with her patience, for Les was being most unreasonable about her slip. 'You've no idea just how great the strain has been,' she added, but although he raised his eyebrows in inquiry she had no intention of elaborating. To inform Les that Scott had known of the deception right from the start would not only throw Les into confusion and embarrassment but would also result in his deep censure and condemnation of her conduct in not being frank with him about the matter. 'When do you propose telling him?' she asked, and he hesitated, frowning heavily.

'It'll have to be soon, now that you've already spilled the beans,' he replied caustically. 'It can't possibly be postponed.'

'You'd have postponed it, if you could?'

He shrugged and said he really didn't know. On thinking about the Shores' position he had in fact felt he must consult them first, and see what they thought about it.

'Of course,' he added, 'I fully intended to tell Gwen the truth, whether I'd decided to postpone telling Scott or not.

Jane left him a few moments later and went to bed. Les had not mentioned anything about his own suspicion that Scott still cared for her, but then he had been fully absorbed by the unwelcome news she had given him.

It was to prove to be another restless night for Jane, and naturally this registered when she arrived at Driftwood House the following morning with dark smudges under her eyes and a pallor in her cheeks. Appearing cool and composed as usual, Scott looked her over for a few seconds before saying,

'You haven't slept, obviously. I hope your concentration isn't going to suffer.'

He sounded heartless, she thought, blinking rapidly.

'I shall do my work with my customary efficiency,' she told him in a tight little voice.

'I'm relieved to hear it. There's a great deal to be done.'

And he worked her harder than ever before. But aside from the almost harsh exterior he exhibited towards her Jane sensed a sort of flatness about him that was totally out of character. He seemed to be fighting some depression of spirits and surging into her mind was the recollection that she had formerly gained the impression that he was a lonely man despite his work and the 'pleasures' to which he had so cynically referred. What had happened to Alma? Jane wondered. Had she finished with Scott? – or had he finished with her?

Jane was musing on these and other questions when Scott's sharp voice brought her back to the fact that she was supposed to be taking a letter.

'Pay attention! You haven't got that last sentence. Read out what you've put down there.'

She swallowed the hard little lump in her throat and obeyed. Silence prevailed for one awful moment after she had finished.

'I'm sorry—' she began. 'If – if you'll repeat—?'

'What's the matter with you?' he demanded, glaring at her. 'What you *have* got down's all wrong!'

She opened her mouth to voice another apology, then closed it again.

Scott drew an exasperated breath, and started again. Jane went off, when she had taken the letter, and typed it out in her own room. She was just getting up with the intention of having it signed when, on glancing out of the window, she saw Scott walking in the garden. It seemed an aimless perambulation, his head being bent and his arms swinging loosely at his sides. Jane's heart contracted, but the next moment she was asking herself why she should be concerned about a man whose treatment of her had resulted in her decision to leave the island of which she had become so fond. It would be a terrible wrench, and it was Scott's fault alone. If he were dejected – and she was sure he was – then his dejection must have something to do with Alma. Perhaps after all he had felt something deeper than mere desire – although not for the life of her could Jane imagine him falling in love with the girl. She was both artificial and affected, and added to this she would never be faithful to Scott – or to any other man she might choose to marry.

Having stood undecided for a few moments Jane went along to Scott's study and placed the letter on his desk. He had said it was important and that he wanted it to catch the next post, which was in less than an hour's time from Bridgetown. However, Jane somehow felt that her intrusion, no matter for what purpose, would be so greatly resented that once again she would feel the lash of his temper. But as she left his room the phone rang and on picking up the receiver she heard a silky female voice say,

'Oh . . . it's you, Miss Coates. Is Scott there? Please tell him I want to speak to him, will you?' To Jane's ears the voice contained a trace of contrition and she instantly assumed there had been a quarrel between the girl and Scott – a lovers' quarrel, she thought, tight-lipped as a sort of bitter contempt caught her for a few seconds.

'He isn't here at the moment,' began Jane, feeling catty enough to leave the girl in suspense.

'Oh, but he must be around somewhere, otherwise you wouldn't be there,' purred Alma. 'Please look for him, Miss Coates.' An order, though silkily given. Jane set her teeth and hesitated.

'I'll see if I can find him,' she said resignedly at last, and put down the receiver.

Scott was nowhere in sight when she stepped out on to the verandah, shaded by a bougainvillaea vine trained up the coral stone pillars and along the roof. He had gone towards a pool formed in the course of a stream and she took the flower-bordered path which led to it. She reached the stream, stopping for an appreciative moment to watch it bubbling and sparkling as it cascaded between tropical plants fringing its banks and spreading over huge coral boulders lying in the bed of the stream. She walked on, passing pools and waterfalls, artificially constructed, but as coral stone was used all the time the result was as natural as if it had been designed by nature's cunning hand, and not by man's at all.

Where could he be? Jane had never been in this part of the grounds before and she stopped again and looked around. Here the gardens began to merge with the acres of woodland which formed the delightful outer perimeter of the estate. She called out eventually and heard a reply. It was a fair way off and she went towards the sugar mill, as it was from that direction Scott's voice had come. A little gasp escaped her as she entered what could only be described as a fairyland of colour and perfume. Huge coral limestone boulders formed a natural rock garden where every kind of exotic plant had been included.

'Oh, how beautiful!' Forgetting the object of her mission, she stopped and stared; a myriad shades of rose and gold, of mauve and pink, met her spellbound gaze. Morning glory and African tulip vied with the exotic passion flower and dazzling flame vine; allamandas spread over the highest boulders, and a fantastic array of orchids contributed their kaleidoscope of colour to the scene of tropical splendour. How lucky Scott was to own such an array of beauty! Jane felt that had she owned these spectacular grounds she would come out here every single day, to wander blissfully among the glorious flowers and trees.

'You were calling?' Scott was at her side, having approached unheard on the soft springy moss growing in the large flat areas between the boulders.

She nodded, still a little dazed by all the splendour around her.

'Miss Bonsall is on the phone,' she informed him.

'Is she?' He appeared not to be in the least interested in Alma just at present. 'You haven't been here before?'

Jane shook her head.

'I didn't even know it existed.'

'I took it for granted you'd have looked around.'

'Only in the gardens near the house. I wouldn't dream of intruding here, unless you invited me to.' She glanced towards the woodlands; wedges of dazzling blue sea could be discerned through a clump of Royal poinciana trees and swaying cabbage palms.

'What makes you think you'd have been intruding? I seem to recall inviting you to look around; we were talking about the monkeys at the time. Have you seen them yet?'

'Not here. I've seen one or two on other parts of the island.' She looked up at him, noticing the little grey lines at the sides of his mouth. There was something tense about the atmosphere which made her say hurriedly, 'Miss Bonsall – aren't you going to answer the telephone?'

He nodded, but absently.

'Yes, I expect so. How long is it since she rang?'

'It must be five minutes – or even more.'

'She's probably rung off, then,' he decided, and an unfathomable silence fell between them as they stood there, side by side, in the beautiful rock garden, with the sound of cascading water drifting to them from the waterfall in the stream which wound into the woodlands before emerging some way off and eventually reaching the sea to mingle its waters with those of the lovely Caribbean.

'I left the letter on your desk,' supplied Jane awkwardly.

'Thank you.' He looked down into her face, twisting a little so that he was in front of her instead of at the side. 'You've no need to be afraid,' he said harshly on seeing her take an involuntary step backwards. 'My ardour's kept for the more romantic atmosphere of the evening.'

She blinked, then stared, eyes wide open.

'That's a very strange remark to make,' she couldn't help saying, and to her added amazement his blue eyes kindled with sudden anger.

'I've come to a decision,' he snapped, and she had the certain impression that he had been been dwelling on this decision – whatever it might be – ever since last night, and that he had come out here this morning, into the grounds of his home, to be alone and ponder over it yet again. 'I've an ultimatum to offer you.'

She started, and her heart jerked. She felt a hint of colour rise in her cheeks. Scott's eyes narrowed and a half-sneer twisted the corners of his mouth.

'There's nothing to blush about,' he assured her in the same harsh tones. 'It's not *that* sort of an ultimatum.'

Jane could only stare, for a moment bereft of speech, fascinated by the swift uncontrollable pulsation of a nerve in his throat.

'Wh-what is it, then?'

'I've decided to overlook the deception, both of your brother and your friends, on one condition.'

'Oh?' was all she could manage, still staring at that nerve and wondering what was to come next. Here was Scott in a totally different mood from any she had encountered before.

'The condition is that you continue working for me.'

'It is—?' Suddenly, like an electric flash across a darkened sky, comprehension dawned, depriving her of breath and speech and affecting every nerve in her body. Dazed by the miracle, she moved her head from side to side and, taking it for a refusal, Scott snarled, eyes blazing,

'In that case, you all go – all!'

Jane came to, and a strange little smile touched her full rosy lips.

'I can't believe it,' she breathed, looking into his eyes with an expression that should have told him all he needed to know but which merely produced puzzlement, to replace the harshness that had settled on the lean angular features. 'It just isn't true. . . .' Overcome, she pressed the tips of her fingers to her eyes, and two great tears escaped and trickled right down to her wrists. 'You wouldn't take it out on David and Susan in any case,' she said, deciding to be practical. 'It isn't like you at all—'

'What the hell are you talking about!' Roughly he gripped her wrists and brought her hands away from her face. 'What are you trying to say?' he demanded. 'Say it and don't go on like that, babbling about the Shores!'

'You're hurting me, Scott—'

'Hurting you! Before I've finished I'll. . . .' His threat was never uttered; he let go of her hands and stared down at her, a slow, triumphant smile dawning as he too managed to see the light at last. 'Jane . . . Jane, my dear. . . .' He too seemed dazed, though not so dazed that he let pass the clear invitation offered by Jane's softly-parted lips. 'My beloved . . . my own girl. How has it happened?'

'It was when you made that threat just now. You were trying to use the situation to get what you wanted – which was for me to stay here. I suddenly grasped the fact that it must be love that led you to such a course, because why else should you be so anxious for me to stay?'

He nodded, admitting that he had given himself away by that threat. He hadn't meant to, though, he told her, not after she had baldly told him she liked Hal Charlton.

'I was madly jealous of him,' continued Scott roughly. 'That's why I ordered you to act in a more seemly manner. I hated the thought that he might be encouraged to make love to you—'

'Oh, but I'd never have let him!'

'I mean – he might have felt he had the right to kiss you.'

'It was a lie anyway,' she confessed. 'I had no feelings whatsoever for him. How could I when I loved you? I merely said I liked him in an effort to stop you from wanting an affair with me.'

'I never did want an affair with you. But I enjoyed frightening you,' he added without a trace of contrition or apology in his voice.

'No – you really never wanted an affair with me?' He shook his head and she accepted this, but went on to say, 'You were punishing me for what I'd done before, weren't you?'

He confessed that this was so.

'My pride had never received such a blow as you gave it when you declared that I had no strength of character, no personality—'

'Don't,' she pleaded. 'I must have been out of my mind to imply such a thing. I know now that you let me have all my own way simply because you loved me so.' She raised her eyes to his and he saw that they were still bright with a film of tears. 'I realized, almost as soon as as I began getting to know you again, just what I'd thrown away. I never even dared to hope that I'd be given a second chance.' Scott said nothing and after a moment she continued, 'I do understand that you should want to punish me, and show me that you could be – be masterful and overbearing, but you needn't have gone so far as to make me believe that you were a rake.'

He made no answer to that and as she watched his expression she knew for sure that he *had* been around since she had sent him away. He had learned all about women in that four years and so his cynicism was not, after all, assumed. Was she disappointed that here was one change that really had taken place? Jane dismissed it from her mind, conscious all at once that it did not matter anyway. It was all in the past; the future was all that now mattered. But she did have to ask if Alma had slept at Driftwood House that night, and she knew an overwhelming sense of relief when he instantly shook his head.

'I'd never any intention of having her sleep here – even in her own apartment,' he added a trifle heartlessly as Jane coloured. 'I was merely endeavouring to make you jealous – in which I failed miserably,' he ended, but now it was Jane's turn to shake her head.

'Haven't I admitted that I very soon began to realize what I'd thrown away?'

'Yes, sweetheart. I forgot.' He drew her into his arms and pressed his lips to hers, tenderly and so very gently, as in the old days. 'I can't bully you, my love,' he said. 'Am I to take it that I'll do as I am?'

For answer she lifted her face again, offering him her lips.

'You certainly put on the act most efficiently,' she said after a long while during which her mouth had become more rosy than ever from his kisses. 'You were cruel!'

He shrugged.

'That was just to show you, my dear, that I'm not really without the ability to master, if I want to.' He paused and his blue eyes glinted. 'I've said I can't ever bully you, but if ever the time comes when you become over-confident about getting all your own way, you'll learn, to your cost, that you have in fact got yourself a master. Remember, I've learned a great deal about women during the past few years, and one important thing is always to know when to draw in the rein.'

Jane changed the subject.

'You know, Scott, although I'd told myself you were acting the way you did in order to get your own back for – for my turning down your offer of marriage, it always seemed—' She stopped for one uncertain moment, endeavouring to find a tactful way of phrasing her words. 'It always seemed quite out of character – as if such conduct was not yours at all.'

He was nodding his head already, even before she had finished speaking.

'And the fact of my reminding you all the while that I had a hold on you?' he supplemented, as if aware that she had meant to include this. 'I just had to keep you here, so that I could try and win your love. I felt that, had I allowed you to tell Les of my knowledge of the deception, both you and he might have left the island. That's what I meant when I said that it didn't suit my purpose for him to be enlightened.'

'I see that now, but it was puzzling at the time.'

'As for my conduct in reminding you I was your employer—'

'Boss,' she put in a little tartly, and Scott laughed.

'All right, sweet, your boss. Well, that was all part of the domineering, masterful pose. I just had to win your love—'

'In that horrid way!' she gasped, and received an amused glance from Scott and the reminder that this was what she had given him to understand was necessary in the man she would eventually marry. 'Oh, dear,' she managed to insert, 'I'll never live it down, I can see that—' Her words were cut as Scott spoke again.

'The man you'd marry must be able to assert himself; he must be possessed of a certain amount of mastery. I can't remember the rest,' he went on, heartlessly immune to her little protesting gestures of the hand. 'Well, my love, I was only giving you what you wanted. Why, then, didn't you respond? I asked myself.'

'I realized,' she offered rather lamely, 'that I really wanted you as you were before.'

'How like a woman! Where do they get their perversity? Not from the spear side, I'll be bound!' Jane said nothing and he added, 'I'm sorry, dear Jane, but it's too late to have me as I was.'

'I know.' But she did add, looking rather coquettishly up at him, 'Nevertheless, there *is* an element of teasing about what you're saying to me.'

'There is?' with a strange, slanting glance that really should have warned her.

'Yes. I know you'll always be gentle with me—' She got no further, the rest being smothered by a kiss that was very, very far from gentle. His arms about her, too, were giving as much pain as pleasure, being as ruthlessly possessive as they were tenderly caressing.

'Scott,' she gasped when at last she was allowed to speak. 'You're crushing me to death! And you said your ardour's kept for the more romantic atmosphere of the evening!'

'And so it is – so beware!' But he was laughing, and he swung her right off the ground and, holding her aloft, looked up with tender emotion into her eyes. 'Dearest Jane—' He put her on her feet. 'My own sweet love! Is this really happening, or is it a dream?' He kissed her, with real tenderness this time and no passion. 'When I awoke this morning I felt as if there wasn't anything to live for, because although I had half decided to threaten you, I knew that if you insisted on turning down my ultimatum I'd never make the others suffer. And what troubled me was that you yourself might just suspect this, in which case my threat would be totally ineffective. But of course, I had no idea that you loved me—' He shook his head. 'Do you know something, darling?'

'We've both been blind.' He nodded and she went on, 'For myself – I've been inordinately stupid, because Les kept on hinting that you cared for me.'

'He did?' Scott was drawing her to him again and it was easy to see that he had little or no interest in Les at this moment.

'Yes. He attached far more importance than I to things like your concern when I hadn't slept— You remember taking me home?' Absently he nodded, caressing her cheek with his lips. 'Then there was the occasion when I ran short of petrol and you took me home again. And there was the occasion when. . . . Darling, are you listening?'

'Hmm . . .?'

Jane gave a happy little laugh and nestled her head against his shoulder. Presently she broke the deep silence.

'I love you, dearest.' The whispered words came like the soft enchanted breath of a summer breeze before, once again, she was swept into the whirlpool of his ardour.